高中生英文寫作錯誤分析與探究

An Analysis of Written Errors in Taiwanese High School Students' Compositions

楊文賢 著

封面設計
實踐大學教務處出版組

出 版 心 語

　　近年來，全球數位出版蓄勢待發，美國從事數位出版的業者超過百家，亞洲數位出版的新勢力也正在起飛，諸如日本、中國大陸都方興未艾，而臺灣卻被視為數位出版的處女地，有極大的開發拓展空間。植基於此，本組自民國 93 年 9 月起，即醞釀規劃以數位出版模式，協助本校專任教師致力於學術出版，以激勵本校研究風氣，提昇教學品質及學術水準。

　　在規劃初期，調查得知秀威資訊科技股份有限公司是採行數位印刷模式並做數位少量隨需出版〔POD＝Print on Demand〕（含編印銷售發行）的科技公司，亦為中華民國政府出版品正式授權的 POD 數位處理中心，尤其該公司可提供「免費學術出版」形式，相當符合本組推展數位出版的立意。隨即與秀威公司密集接洽，出版部李協理坤城數度親至本組開會討論，雙方就數位出版服務要點、數位出版申請作業流程、出版發行合約書以及出版合作備忘錄等相關事宜逐一審慎研擬，歷時 9 個月，至民國 94 年 6 月始告順利簽核公布。

這段期間，承蒙本校謝前校長孟雄、謝副校長宗興、王教務長又鵬、藍教授秀璋以及秀威公司宋總經理政坤等多位長官給予本組全力的支持與指導，本校多位教師亦不時從旁鼓勵與祝福，在此一併致上最誠摯的謝意。本校新任校長張博士光正甫上任（民國 94 年 8 月），獲知本組推出全國大專院校首創的數位出版服務，深表肯定與期許。諸般溫馨滿溢，將是挹注本組持續推展數位出版的最大動力。

　　本出版團隊由葉立誠組長、王雯珊老師、賴怡勳老師三人為組合，以極其有限的人力，充分發揮高效能的團隊精神，合作無間，各司統籌策劃、協商研擬、視覺設計等職掌，在精益求精的前提下，至望弘揚本校實踐大學的校譽，具體落實出版機能。

實踐大學教務處出版組　謹識

中華民國 94 年 10 月

自序

臺灣高中生的英文寫作能力大幅下降已經是不爭的事實。這可由每年大學指定科目考試中的英文作文皆有數萬考生得零分,和全民英檢中的寫作能力通過率甚低中看出端倪。再者,加上臺灣的高中英文老師大部分也把教英文寫作視為一件苦差事,兩個因素交互影響之下,著實令人不免擔憂將來我們的高中生是否能夠再提起筆寫一篇最基本的英文文章。

由於一些教師和學生對於近年盛行於英語教學界的「溝通式教學法」產生一番誤解,其認為「溝通為上、形式為次」或「流暢度應甚於正確度」,以致於英語口語和書寫的使用上流於「不求甚解、不拘小節」之層面。這些對於「溝通式教學法」的誤解可說是造成了現今臺灣學生使用英文上的正確性明顯低落的其中一項主要原因。

雖說在老師的要求和考試的雙重壓力下,學生也都極力地想避免犯英文寫作上的錯誤,但努力卻往往適得其反,以致於對於寫作產生無比的壓力,對於錯誤感到莫名的恐懼,最終將對英文寫作完全失去動機和興趣,這將不是我們所樂見的情形。當然,「錯誤」應該被改正,但它絕對不是代表「罪惡」,不管是老師或者是學生,在追求語意或文法的流暢性和正確度的同時,應將「犯錯」視為「學習者正在測試其獨特的學習假設之必經歷程」;在追求完美的結果之前也應該改採一個更寬容的心態去面對「犯錯過程」。畢竟,英文寫作是一個既注重「過程」也看重「結果」的一種教學活動。

本書即針對目前臺灣高中生的英文寫作歷程作一番深入的探討。書中透過寫作樣本分析、問卷和訪談的方式來（一）歸類和計算出臺灣高中生常犯的英文寫作錯誤種類和頻率，並試圖提出可能造成犯錯的合理解釋；（二）分析學生對於其英文寫作過程中所犯之寫作錯誤的心理態度；（三）了解現職英文老師在傾聽完學生的想法和態度後的另一番見解。

　　研究中發現臺灣學生的英文寫作的確在語意的表達上不求甚解，甚至充滿中文化的使用和思考邏輯，在文法的使用精確度上也亟需加強，且內容上也嫌創意和深度不足。然者，研究中也發現學生對於寫作「錯誤」的態度從以往的「欲除之而後快」逐漸轉化成是一種代表測試個人學習假設的必經歷程。這些發現著實可為現今的英文作文教學帶來另一種新視野、新態度和新方法。

　　能教導學生寫出一篇文情並茂、合「理」合「法」的英文作文是所有臺灣高中英文老師的目標和責任，但「人非聖賢、孰能無過」，期盼透過本書，老師能夠更深入地認識學生所犯錯誤的類型和原因，並體會學生在寫作上所承受的心理壓力，進而在寫作教學法上有所調整而精進。

　　最後，感謝所有參與的老師和學生得以使本研究順利完成；並感謝實踐大學的鼎力支持，和教務處出版組同仁的辛勤校對和設計工作，使本書能順利付梓。萬分感謝！

作者 楊文賢

中華民國 94 年 12 月

ABSTRACT

In this study, about 360 senior high school students in different grades from three different schools in Taiwan are the main participants together with a number of English teachers involved in the research. The 45 samples are selected from 360 short compositions written by the students, the 113 questionnaires collected from the students, and the interviews conducted with English teachers are the sources of data analysis for this study.

The study applies two different methods in analysing the data. The first one is Error Analysis which is used to analyse the categorises and distributions of writing errors by the students and this can detect their writing strategies and writing difficulties they may confront in the process of writing English compositions. The second one is Questionnaire Analysis based on interpretative method which investigates the students' attitudes and perceptions towards the written errors they made. Hopefully, this two-stages analysis can help not only students in realising the possible reasons which cause written errors and raising their critical thinking about errors but also teachers in appreciating the errors their students make and then adopting different methods in teaching writing effectively.

The book consists of five chapters. Chapter One is a general introduction about the study together with definitions of a

CONTENTS

number of basic terms concerning about error analysis. Chapter Two provide a number of related literature reviews on Contrastive Analysis (CA), Error Analysis (EA), Interlanguage, and error treatment. In addition, the outcomes from previous research related to this study and books concerned with how to teach writing are reviewed in this chapter as well. Chapter Three present a short introduction to the methodology and research procedures applied in this study. This includes research aims, the participants, the research instruments, and the likely limitations of this study. Chapter Four is the main focus of this book, consisting of the data analysis and discussion of the three stages. A number of significant findings and pedagogical implications generated from the research also can be found in this main chapter. Chapter Five briefly concludes this study.

To sum up, the students' writing ability should be improved without doubt, especially in the aspects of grammar, semantics, and word selection. English teachers should notice the potential influence from the mother tongue and the target language in the process of the students' English writing. Furthermore, both teachers and learners are encouraged to take a more positive attitude towards writing errors. They have to realise that errors represent a process of learning i.e. learners are testing their hypothesis about the language and making sense of their learning.

高中生英文寫作錯誤分析與探究

An Analysis of Written Errors in Taiwanese High School Students' Compositions

contents

出版心語
自序
ABSTRACT

CONTENTS

CHAPTER 3

METHODOLOGY

CHAPTER 4

FINDINGS, DISCUSSION, AND IMPLICATIONS

CHAPTER 5

CONCLUSION   140

REFERENCES   142

APPENDIX   148

CHAPTER 1
INTRODUCTION

1.1 Introduction

1.2 Definitions of Terms

CHAPTER 1

INTRODUCTION

1.1 Introduction

For English learners, it is very natural to make errors. Even when we are using our native language, we cannot avoid making errors, either. Native speakers can always know consciously where they went wrong and how to correct these errors. Their errors usually refer to a lack of attention or a slip in performance. However, for non-native English learners, rarely can they consciously correct their language errors. It is likely that they cannot detect whether they have made mistakes. Even if they are aware of their errors, they might not be capable of dealing with them. This reflects a lack of English competence. Hence, in the view of linguistic psychology, the errors made by native speakers and non-native speakers are very distinctive from each other.

Nowadays language learners' errors are not usually thought as an unforgivable sin any more. Errors could be valuable for teachers to know if learners have acquired what they need to know or where they have difficulties in learning a language. Furthermore, analysing these errors also provides teachers with information to feed into their teaching methods. We thus can say both learners and teachers would definitely benefit from learners' errors.

If teachers do hope to gain some insights from learners' errors either in changing their attitudes towards errors or adjusting the teaching methods, it could be of help to analyse learners' errors first. This is what I aim to do in this study. However, there are too many different kinds of errors, and it would be impossible to explore each of them. Therefore, in this study I will only focus on the writing errors made by Taiwanese high school students.

"Writing" is exactly what most EFL students are afraid of. Since 1981, it has been compulsory for Taiwanese high school students to compose a short English composition in the Joint University Entrance Examination. Due to this, English writing has become another focus in English language teaching in Taiwan recently. However, how to treat learners' writing errors in English seems to be a dilemma for many English teachers in Taiwan. This raises a number of questions concerning teaching in Taiwan:

- Are we supposed to correct each writing error?
- Can we have more tolerant attitudes towards these writing errors?
- How do our learners view their own errors?
- What are the students' expectations from us in dealing with their errors?

The answers to the above questions should provide some useful insights for English teachers in Taiwan. Hopefully, this study can provide sufficient answers to the questions.

In the structure of this study, firstly I tried to analyse Taiwanese high school students' writing errors by using the method of error analysis. Secondly, the focus shifted to students themselves. I explored students' writing process and their attitudes towards errors and error correction. The aim of this second part is to know if there is a perceptional gap between teachers and students about errors. Finally, I interviewed three English teachers from Taiwan in order to have a more objective understanding towards writing errors and error treatment.

1.2 Definitions of Terms

In this section, the definitions of some basic terms appearing in the rest of the paper will be defined as follows.

<u>Contrastive Analysis (CA)</u>

CA is a systematic comparison of the source language/ L1 (native language of the learner) and the target language/ L2 (language to be taught) at all levels of structure, which will generate predictions about areas of learning difficulty in the target language for the speakers of the source language (Chen, 1979).

Error Analysis (EA)

EA is a careful study of a large corpus of errors committed by speakers of the source language attempting to express them i.e. selves in the target language, which provides factual data rather than theoretical speculations, for developing a syllabus or a model of second language acquisition (Chen, 1979).

Interlanguage

Coined by Selinker (1972), Interlanguage means a special individual type of language produced by ESL/EFL learners who are in the process of learning a language, and learners would produce a series of Interlanguages as they learn.

Taiwanese vs. Chinese

In this study, Taiwanese refers to those who live in Taiwan while Chinese means the official language used by the people living in Taiwan, also known as Mandarin.

Transfer

Transfer means the effect of one language on the learning of another language. It can be divided into negative transfer, also called interference, and positive transfer. Negative transfer means that a language learner applies what he/she has known in the native language to the unknown target language, which leads to an error. For example, a Chinese-speaking learner of English may produce the incorrect sentence *I tomorrow will go see movie* instead of *I will go to see a movie tomorrow.* While positive transfer can make learning easier, especially when the native language and the target language share the same form or meaning. For instance, the meaning of *"blueprint"* is not difficult for Chinese-speaking English learners at all because there is an equivalent meaning in Chinese, 藍圖 (lan-tu).

Overgeneralization

While learning a language, a learner extends the use of a grammatical rule or linguistic item beyond its accepted usage, usually by making words or structures follow a more regular pattern (Richards, 1998). For example, a learner may use *"mans"* instead of *"men"* for the plural of *man* and *"goed"* instead of *"went"* for the past tense of *go*.

Simplification

Simplification is used to describe what happens when learners make use of rules which are grammatically less complex than the target language rules (Richards, 1998). For example, a leaner may use "I look forward to see you very soon." instead of "I look forward to seeing you very soon." because he/she simplifies the rule, "use the bare verb after a 'to'", and does not notice its restriction. This often results from an overgeneralisation.

Competence error vs. Performance error

Competence error is used to mean an error made due to the learner's lack of linguistic knowledge about the target language, while performance error refers to an error resulting from fatigue, excitement, nervousness, or the lack of attention.

Interlingual error vs. Intralingual error

An interlingual error is an error which results from language transfer, i.e. it is caused by the learner's native language (Richards, 1998). For instance, this incorrect English sentence *"Mary today is sick"*, produced simply based on the word order of Chinese, takes place of the correct English sentence *"Mary is sick today."* However, an intralingual error is one resulting form faulty or partial learning of the target language, rather than from language transfer. It may be committed by the influence of one target language item upon another (Richards, 1998). For example, a learner of English may produce a sentence like *"She is sleeps."* because he/she mixes up the structures *"She is sleeping."* and *"She sleeps."*

Global error vs. Local error

A global error refers to the misuse of a structure that would damage or breakdown the communication and thus the meaning is difficult or impossible to be understood, such as *"My friend hurry up so that we are late for school in order to catch a bus."*

However in contrast, a misuse of a structure that does not lead to the difficulty of comprehension is named a local error. "If I got up earlier, I will not be late." provides an example.

CHAPTER 2

LITERATURE REVIEW

In this following section, literature concerning contrast analysis (CA), error analysis (EA), interlanguage, errors, error treatment, writing errors made by Taiwanese students and how to teach English writing will be discussed respectively.

2.1 Contrast Analysis (CA)

In 1945, in *Teaching and Learning English as a Foreign Language*, Charles Fries initiated the development of CA. He writes that

> the most effective materials are those that are
> based upon a scientific description of the language
> to be learned, carefully compared with a parallel
> description of the native language of the learner.
> (Fries, 1945: 9)

However, it is Lado that expands and classifies CA. In his classic, *Linguistics Across Cultures,* Lado (1976) claims that by comparing a learner's native language with target language, we can predict and describe the patterns that will cause difficulties to learners. He continues that after the comparison, if the structures between two languages are similar, then they will be easy to learn because these structures will be transferred to the target language; on the contrary, if different, learners will have difficulty in learning the target language. CA would try to attribute most learning difficulties to the transfer from learners' native language, and converge those language errors on the influence of mother tongue. CA even asserts that nearly up to 30% of errors in language learning can be traced back to the interference of one's mother tongue.

Yet as evidence shows, CA could only be the most predictive at the level of phonology while in other aspects of language, syntactic, semantic, or lexical interference is a far less successful predictor. This is because errors predicted did not materialise in target language, or errors did appear there but CA had not predicted in advance (James, 1998: 4). Even CA is more predictive in phonological aspect; yet, a language constitutes hundreds of thousands of items and it is impossible to predict difficulty beyond some very glaring phonological difference between two different languages (Brown, 1987). Most important of all, many teachers regarded CA as useless and rejected it for CA does not offer any pedagogical methodology in language teaching. What CA does is just the process of making predictions but no linguistic explanation for known errors can be seen.

It is because CA has been widely questioned that Wardhaugh (1970) proposes CA should have two different versions. One is the strong version, maintaining that CA can predict points that will cause difficulties and those that will cause no difficulties; yet, this version has been testified as unrealistic and impracticable. The other is the weak version, which states that linguists should use knowledge, which is available to them to give an account of the observed difficulties only. At present, it is the weak version that still has certain possibilities for usefulness.

2.2 Error Analysis

Being able to detect students' learning difficulties has been a major concern in the realm of English language teaching. After World War II, Contrastive Analysis (CA) was introduced by Fries and used by Lado. CA was once regarded as panacea to predict most language errors and then cure all of them. However, evidence shows that CA could be the most predictive at the level of phonology but less predictive at the level of syntax (Richards, 1974). Evidently it may be impossible to contrast two different languages in a short period of time, and then expect to predict all kinds of language errors students would make. Furthermore, not each language error can be attributed to the differences between the mother tongue and the target language as CA claimed.

In order to analyse students' difficulties in language learning more meaningfully, Corder proposed trying to understand errors from the perspective of psycholinguistics. Applied linguists use error analysis to study learners' language errors in order to explain their possible causes (Corder, 1981).

In the following sections, the aims, nature, and limitations of EA and Interlanguage will be discussed in order.

2.2.1 Nature of error analysis

When CA (Contrast Analysis) was found to be full of pitfalls, many linguists altered the focus of their concern. They collect students' errors and then analyse these errors directly. This research methodology is known as error analysis (EA). Therefore, basically speaking, EA is a reaction towards CA. Just as Corder acutely points out, the assumption of negative transfer should be replaced with the assumption of the learner as a generator of generalisations about the target language (Dulay & Burt, 1974).

2.2.2 The purposes of error analysis

The purpose of using EA may vary, depending on who does the research. For linguists, they hope to discover the process and learning strategies used by language learners. However, for educators or language teachers, they hope EA can help them realise what language difficulties students would face in the classroom. Then according to these difficulties, teachers can design remedial teaching and a teaching syllabus.

2.2.3 The procedure of error analysis

Once the errors have been collected, EA can be divided

into the following stages (Tso, 1993; James, 1998).

(1) Identifying errors: to find out errors from students' output.

(2) Describing errors: to point out under which situation do students commit such errors. The purpose of describing errors is to justify learners' intuitions and to create categories.

(3) Classifying errors: to categorise students' errors on the basis of some taxonomy.

(4) Counting errors: to calculate students' error frequency either in absolute or relative frequency.

(5) Interpreting errors: to account for why learners would commit such errors.

(6) Evaluating errors: to understand to what extent those errors would block learners' communication.

2.2.4 The problems and limitations of error analysis

To begin with, it may be sometimes difficult to identify errors. For example, some global errors (referring to the language errors which are serious enough to damage the communication) may mix together with the sentence or larger unit of text that contains them and thus are difficult to identify. Also, language is changing all the time and what is defined as an error today may become acceptable tomorrow.

Secondly, in classifying errors, it is always difficult to categorise each error into its right place for one reason may easily overlap with another. Besides, what makes classification harder is that there still has been no criterion for a taxonomy so far. Moreover, in accounting for errors, if one error just appears continually, how to calculate its frequency is a big puzzle.

Next, in interpreting errors, different interpretations are inevitably so subjective that they lead to much criticism. An interpretation on points of difficulty in the target language may be various depending on different correctors. This means different people identify different reasons for the same error (Schachter & Celce-Murcia, 1971).

Furthermore, in EA, teachers tend to be preoccupied with noticing errors where the production of correct language is often neglected (Brown, 1987; Chaudron, 1977). In fact, students would be strongly encouraged if teachers can notice their accurate production, not only the errors. EA keeps teachers "too focused on specific languages rather than viewing universal aspects of language" (Brown, 1987: 172). Some elements of learners' language are reflected neither from the target language nor the native language.

Finally, Schacter (1974), based on her study investigating English relative clauses used by Chinese, Japanese, Persian, and Arabic speakers, finds that EA has a fundamental flaw:

> a failure to recognise that learners have a tendency
> to avoid target language item they are not sure
> about, and so not to commit errors which they
> would be expected to commit (Schacter, 1974: 18).

Although EA in itself has some problems and limitations, yet we cannot deny its contribution to language teaching. It not only gives teachers "an idea about how students are progressing and indicate any points which have generally not been learned" (Norrish, 1995:97), but it is also contributive to designing teaching courses.

2.3 Literature Review on Interlanguage

Learners also make mistakes from trying out rules in the new language, thus creating their own version of the language. Selinker (1972) defines this as "interlanguage". Interlanguage refers to a sort of language produced by language learners who are learning a language. This individualised and specific language is different from both the target language and the native language.

Corder (1981) termed this phenomenon as "idiosyncratic dialect". It means some rules governing the dialect cannot be found in any social dialect but only belong to learners themselves. These rules are normally unstable and not readily interpretable. He (Corder, 1981) strongly claims that unless we have got enough information about learners' idiosyncratic dialect we cannot term it as learners' erroneous, deviant or ill-formed rules. In addition, "approximative system" is another term created by Nemser (1971) to identify those special rules employed by the learners in an attempt to operate the target language.

However the three terms differ from each other, they all share the same concept: second/foreign language learners are developing their own self-contained linguistic system, which is neither the same as the target language nor to the native language. Moreover, this peculiar language could be very "permeable (not fixed, but open to amendment), dynamic (constantly changing) and systematic (predictable through detecting learners' using these rules" (Ellis, 1995a).

Interlanguage theory enlightens language teachers that there is still another source causing "errors". However, it is interesting and debatable to know if corrections to the interlanguage would lead to a progress in the language learning.

In conclusion, EA and interlanguage both have different methods to view errors, and lead to different attitudes towards errors and different views regarding the influence from the mother tongue in language learning, but at least they share the same goal - - to understand the process of the target language learning.

2.4 Errors and Error Treatment

Nowadays, learners' errors are not necessarily regarded as something to be avoided at all costs. On the contrary, errors can be viewed as a necessary and useful process in learning a language. Just as Norrish (1995: 113) proposes, error is not only inevitable, but "there are strong reasons for believing it to be an essential part of learning, in that it aids the learner and provides him with feedback in the process of concept formation."

During the past few decades, applied linguists have abandoned the view that language learning is a formation of a habit, and errors are not necessarily regarded as a bad habit (Huang, 1983). Contrarily, learning a language is generally thought of as a complicated cognitive process, and errors could serve as a precious resource to probe the learning process.

The following section will be divided into six categories concerning the sources of errors, the classifications of errors, the values of errors, another source of errors, the priority of error correction, and the effectiveness of error correction.

2.4.1 The sources of errors

Where language errors come from is a potentially important issue because once the sources of errors can be identified then the design of treatment to reduce errors is more likely. Different views towards the sources are presented as follows.

First, George (1972) asserts that the three principal causes of errors are: redundancy of the code, unsuitable presentation in class and several sorts of interference. Richards (1974) explains the possible reasons as language transfer from the native language, intralingual interference from the target language along with different sociolinguistic situations.

However, Taylor (in Ellis, 1994) identifies four different sources of errors on the basis of a broader view:

- psycholinguistic sources, the difficulty of production,
- sociolinguistic sources, the difficulty in adjusting language in accordance with social context,
- epistemic source, learner's lack of knowledge,
- and discourse sources, problems in the organisation of information into a coherent text.

Norrish (1995) comes up with more different sources, and concludes that errors may result from learners' carelessness, interference from L1/L2, direct translation from the native language, different interpretations between learners and teachers, the false analogy due to ignorance of rule restrictions and learners' own predictions towards the unknown.

From the perspective of psycholinguistics, Johnson (1996) offers two reasons to explain why learners make errors. One is that students do not have the appropriate declarative knowledge or maybe they have the wrong knowledge. The other is students lack procedural knowledge of processing knowledge. In other words, it is not a problem of faulty linguistic knowledge but learners' difficulty in operating their competence rightly.

Finally, James (1998: 175) identifies the sources from learners' ignorance and avoidance, and interference from either the native language or the target language. Therefore, it could be concluded from his discussion that the sources of errors fall into three main divisions: slip of pen/tongue, and interference from L1 and L2. In a word, there may be many possible reasons causing errors and thus teachers need to be aware of where the error may come from when treating students' writing errors.

2.4.2 The classifications of errors

In EA, the classification of errors seems to be the toughest task since one error may easily overlap with another. This perhaps is the reason why there still has been no standard and ideal taxonomy of language errors so far. Burt and Kiparsky (1972) propose that errors could be differentiated into global errors and local errors. Global errors refer to the misuse of structure and thus damage or breakdown communication. For example, conjunction errors, which involve the overall meaning of the sentence and major constituent classes of the sentence or transformations, will seriously influence comprehension of sentences (Lee, 1997). Local errors (referring to errors which will not damage communication) such as lexical errors, noun errors, and adverbs, etc. do not usually cause major problems in comprehension. However, the distinction between global errors and local errors is sometimes vague. For instance, though a global error is found in a student's writing, yet due to the familiarity between the teacher and the student, the teacher still can guess what the student tries to convey and thus ignore its seriousness. However, this error may possibly breakdown communication for other readers.

Politzer and Ramirez (1973) create a different linguistic taxonomy: morphological category and syntax category, under which three main subcategories are based on different parts of speech or parts of the sentence. However, they clarify the purpose of this categorization just as an aid to present their data.

In addition, Richards (1974) divides language errors into three main groups: intralingual errors (errors within the target language), interlingual errors (errors between the target language and the native language), and developmental errors. However, classifying an error as an interlingual error or an intralingual one is still very difficult. For example, the misuse of the article in "I have been to the America twice." could be attributed to an interlingual error (there is no obvious article usage in Chinese) (Yang, 2004) or the intralingual error (the overgeneralisation of the article usage).

Furthermore, Deng (1987) categorises errors into three main groups: performance errors, intralingual errors, and interlingual errors according to an investigation of tense errors made by third year senior high school students. This grouping is nearly the same as that of Richards'.

Huang (1988) brings in another element, the rhetorical or discoursal aspect, and classifies all the linguistic errors into three types: lexical, grammatical (or syntactic), and rhetorical. Similarly, in Chiang, P. J.'s (1993) thesis, errors are grouped into three main divisions: the lexical, the grammatical (or syntactic) and the semantic, rhetorical and stylistic. Similarly, subcategories and sub-subcategories are subsumed under each main heading.

Lee (1997) synthesises Chiang's ideas (1993) with Huang's (1986) in his own study. "All the errors were to be classified into three major categories: lexical errors, grammatical errors, and semantic" (Lee, 1997: 43). Those errors that cannot be categorised into any of the above will be termed miscellaneous errors. Subcategories under each main heading are further listed. In this study, I adopted this categorisation to analyse the sampled compositions for it caters for both grammatical and semantic aspects.

Finally, Chiang, H. H. (1999) selects the main errors made by Taiwanese students and classifies those into three categories: errors in verbal groups, errors in nominal groups, and errors in prepositional groups depending on functional grammar. Chiang, H. H.'s classification is very unique compared with the former ones for it is the only one that adopts the viewpoints from functional grammar. However, it neglects the discoursal and rhetorical aspects of language.

In fact, no categorisation could be labelled as the perfect one. This is why it would be useful to establish a standard taxonomy for classifying errors in order not to get confused with the classification of errors any more.

2.4.3 The value of errors

When talking about errors, Brooks (1964: 58) states, "like sin, error is to be avoided and its influence overcome." His solution to errors is offering students more practice and drills. However, after the 1960s, such a viewpoint has been questioned extensively. Many assertions about errors have become more positive. For example, Corder (1967: 25) says, "error can be beneficial for the teacher, the researcher and the learner." Errors help teachers evaluate to what extent a learner has progressed, they provide researchers with evidence of how language is learnt, and they help students to form their hypotheses about the language. Moreover, he also claims errors can

> allow the learner's innate strategies to *dictate our (teachers' and educators') practice* and *determine our syllabus*, and thus teachers and educators can learn to *adapt themselves to the learner's needs* rather than impose upon him *their* preconceptions of *how* he/she ought to learn, *what* he/she ought to learn and *when* he/she ought to learn it (Corder, 1967: 27).

Indeed, errors themselves are essential and also useful. This is not only because errors are "signals that our learners are successfully learning the language i.e. they are taking necessary learning steps," (Edge, 1989: 13) but also because they help teachers understand the process of language learning, design the teaching syllabus and provide clues to how to lead learners from limited schemata to more generalised ones. Errors are learners' predictions about their learning and it is the teachers' responsibility to respect and encourage these predictions (George, 1972; Jain, 1974; Brown, 1987; Edge, 1989; Norrish, 1995).

Learners should be taught to express their affection, attitudes, or perceptions by using English. "Language is not a set of facts to be learned but a medium for expressing thoughts, feelings and communicating with other people" (Norrish, 1995: 2). This proposition has a great influence on deciding the objectives, materials, and methodologies in teaching English. For example, in March 1994 (Huang, 1983: 109), the national curriculum of teaching English in senior high school in Taiwan abandoned the demand that students should use pure and authentic English. On the contrary, it puts stress on students' expressing their thoughts as freely as possible. This is because errors could not be avoided completely in learning English.

2.4.4 Another source of errors

In a TEFL (teaching English as a foreign language) context such as Taiwan, "the error in the foreign language situation really has to be a result of something that happens in the classroom" (Norrish, 1995: 37). It has been long assumed by English teachers that almost all errors result from learners themselves. However, in fact not all errors come from learners but surprisingly some may be caused by teachers and textbooks. These are called "induced errors". Stenson (1974) defines those errors resulting from the classroom situation rather than from students' incomplete linguistic competence or interference form their mother tongue as "the induced error". For example, teachers' mis-instruction, faulty presentation of a structure or word in a textbook, or a pattern that is rotely memorised by drills but not properly contextualised may result in induced errors (Stenson, 1974; Ellis, 1995b). Senior high school students of Taiwan tend to memorise those so-called 'model compositions' and patterns without knowing if the pattern is appropriately used or not. Thus, it is common to read works with perfect patterns but with poor content.

2.4.5 The priorities of error treatment

What kinds of errors should be treated immediately? What kinds of errors can be dealt with later and what kinds of errors could be just ignored? The answers to these questions can help teachers to decrease their burden of correcting writing errors and also help students gain confidence in writing for they will not see the returned compositions covered with red corrections. Olsson (in Norrish, 1995: 107) points out an error whose form is unacceptable and thus blocks comprehension should be treated with high priority. However, if an error is unacceptable in form but does not result in readers' irritation, then no immediate treatment is needed. In addition, Cohen (1975: 414) lists six types of errors needed to be treated immediately. They are

1. errors affecting intelligibility such as global errors or semantic errors,
2. high-frequency errors,
3. errors at a high level of generality,
4. errors with stigmatizing or irritating effects,
5. errors affecting a large percent of the students,
6. and errors relevant to the pedagogic focus.

Additionally, Ellis (1995a: 54-55) makes the important distinction view towards error treatment between mistakes and errors made by students. If students make mistakes, then students should be encouraged to correct those by themselves. For example, "bad mood", "carelessness", or "fatigue" will undoubtedly interfere with language production. Errors resulting from these factors should be left for students to cope with. However, teachers should take responsibility for dealing with the linguistic or communicative errors in teaching. Secondly, global errors should be corrected more urgently than local errors for the former would breakdown communication easily.

To sum up, correcting the errors which affect the overall comprehension is more urgent. Next, correct stigmatised errors for these can involve highly negative response from native speakers. *"I never don't walk to school when it is raining."* (double negatives) is an example. Finally, correct the errors which relate to the learner's next stage in language development. Here is an example. The sentence *"If I am a bird, I will fly in the sky."* should be corrected if the next pedagogical focus is the pattern like *"If I were a bird, I would...."*

2.4.6 The effectiveness of error correction

Teachers would like to know if students will not make the same error any more after correcting it. *Is it worthwhile and effective to correct students' errors?* Some think only content words need correction while some agree to correct each linguistic error (Ellis, 1995b: 72). Those who view error correction in language learning as necessary claim that this could help students to discover the functions and limitations of the target language, and to achieve greater accuracy in production finally (Henderickson, 1978; Lightbown, 1990; Fathman & Whalley, 1990). In Cathcart & Olsen's study (1976), they find that learners hope each error can be corrected. Moreover, James (1998: 243-248) proposes that some students especially need correction, such as the careful planners who will not risk self-correction, learners processing difficult language, and the students learning a language as a foreign language. This is because they receive much less correction outside the classroom compared with a learner's learning a language as a second language.

However, some linguists have taken a position against overemphasising error-correction. Corder (1967, 1984) says error correction is less instructive to both learners and teachers, and it simply provides negative evidence necessary to discover so-called correct concepts and rules. In addition, Dulay, Burt and Krashen (James, 1998: 243-248) express the view that correction cannot change the order of acquisition of target language items " based on evidence that it does not work with children acquiring the L1, and does not work in untutored L2 acquisition contexts."

Seriously speaking, error correction still has its own advantages, especially for those students learning English as a foreign language, like Taiwanese students. When I examine the status of English teaching and learning in Taiwan, I agree with what Norrish (1995: 97) states: "if the teacher were to pay no attention at all to the learners' errors, then the students' chances of success in examinations would obviously be reduced." Under such learning circumstance, teachers in Taiwan seem to be the main providers of correct language usage then. With no doubts, many humanistic viewpoints towards errors and error treatment are indeed valuable but "contextual difference" should be also taken into consideration.

2.5 Literature Review on Written Errors Made by Taiwanese Students

In this section, the outcomes of previous research investigating English writing problems confronted by Taiwanese students are described.

First of all, Huang (1974) used university students in Taiwan to examine the grammatical problems that they may have while writing English compositions. He found that the hierarchy of difficulty in their grammatical problems is verbs, articles, nouns, and prepositions.

Next, in 1979, Chen, in his Ph. D. dissertation, divided the errors made by the English-major students in National Kaohsiung Normal University into local errors and global errors. The hierarchy of frequency and difficulty was found to be as follows: verbs, nouns, global errors, determiners, prepositions, adjectives, spelling errors, and pronouns.

Then, in Chiang's study (1981), the writing errors made by English-major students in National Taiwan Normal University were categorised on the basis of traditional grammar into three types: lexical, grammatical, and semantic errors. She found that the hierarchy of difficulty was verbs, nouns, articles, prepositions, adjectives and adverbs, punctuation, conjunctions, and pronouns.

In 1987, Ying collected one hundred and twenty compositions from five senior high schools in Kaohsiung to investigate the learners' interlangauge. She classified the errors into three categories: overgeneralisation of the target language, simplification, and transfer from the native language. She found that errors resulting from the mother tongue interference accounted for 78.9% of the errors, among which word order, lexicon, tenses, conjunctions, articles, and prepositions were the order of difficulty. Ying (1987) concluded that it was the strategy of language transfer that is used most by high school students. What Ying found either in the order of difficulty or in the reasons of errors is significantly different from that of Chiang.

In the next year, Huang (1988) assembled students' compositions from the high-ranking senior high schools all over Taiwan. He came to the conclusion that grammatical errors, which constituted 72.91% of all the errors, still posted the most difficult problem for these advanced learners.

In her survey, Chiang (1993) graded the hierarchy of writing difficulty between the elementary group and intermediate group. She discovered that the elementary group made errors in the following order: conjunctions, subjects, run-on sentences, subjects, and complement while the hierarchy of difficulty in the intermediate group was run-on sentences, conjunctions, subjects, objects and complements. She arrived at the conclusion that the difference of hierarchies between these two groups might result from their applying different strategies while writing.

Lee (1997) examined the problem of English writing from forty sophomore cadets and senior cadets in a military school in Taiwan and found that subjects make 10.1 errors out of every hundred words on average. The result led to the conclusion that due to the lack of sufficient linguistic competence, intralinguistic transfer, and interlinguistic transfer, these cadets had more problems in subordination construction. The hierarchy of error frequency-- grammar, lexicon, and semantics-- was similar to the above outcomes.

Recently, Chiang (1999) conducted research into secondary school students' writing problems based on the perspective of functional grammar. Finally, he concluded that the tense usage in a verbal group was the most difficult for them. He explained the reason as follows.

> In English, the verbal groups signify the primary as well as secondary tense; however, in Chinese they are indicated by the context temporal adjuncts or particles (Chiang, 1999).

He concluded that interlanguage is the major influence causing errors.

To sum up, most of the above findings indicate that grammatical errors are still the most common problem for Taiwanese students.

2.6 Literature on How to Teach English Writing

In fact, there are quite a few important books discussing how to deal with errors when teaching students writing but it is very unlikely to include all of them in this section. Therefore, only three key books are summarised below.

To begin with, Robinson (1969) points out that in order to decrease students' writing errors, teachers had better prepare guided writings for students to complete, in which transformation, insertion, completion, and oral practice may be the choices. Besides, students should also be given enough repeated practice of certain patterns before writing. Moreover, she argues it is a teacher's job to create an atmosphere for students to write without fear but with confidence. This is a principle worth remembering and other writers have suggested how it might work in practice.

Next, White (1986) in his book, *Teaching Written English*, groups English writing into seven different types, narrative writing, description of objects, description of people, description of paces, description of processes, writing of recommending, and questions and answers for both personal and institutional writing. In the book, he offers teachers some guidelines to how to teach each type of writing. Also, White (1986) emphasises that teachers should encourage students to write simple and accurate sentences rather than complex but inaccurate ones and to be confident in this before moving on.

Finally, Norrish (1995) offers some guidelines to how to teach English writing as well. He (1995: 63) recommends that students should be allowed to do free writing only when they are ready i.e. they have sufficient linguistic competence and concept formation, and thirdly in the beginning stage of writing, providing too many guidance or practices students are not ready for yet is not ideal.

In fact, there are indeed numerous literatures concerning about the above topics; however, due to the space limitation only a number of significant ones related to this study were selected. These above writings have influenced the recommendations made later in this study.

CHAPTER 3

METHODOLOGY

3.1. Research Aims

3.2. Research Participants and Methods

3.3. Limitations of the Study

CHAPTER 3

METHODOLOGY

The following section is about the research aims, the participants, research methods and limitations of this study.

3.1 Research Aims

In this study, there are two main aims. Firstly, I hope to identify different writing errors at the level of accuracy demonstrated by different grade students in senior high school, and then to find the reasons for these errors. Almost no attempts, so far, have been made to investigate writing ability among three different grades (freshman, junior, and senior) in senior high school in Taiwan. Therefore, the sub-divided objectives of this aim are:

- to categorise Taiwanese students' writing errors on the basis of the accuracy in writing,
- to give some account of students' errors, interference from the mother tongue and the target language,
- and finally to provide some pedagogical implications, derived from the findings of this study, for English teachers to teach writing effectively.

The second aim is to examine students' attitudes towards their own errors and their expectations regarding error treatment.

I should also compare these with teachers' attitudes, and comments on any contextual factors influencing the error treatment from the interview.

3.2 Research Participants and Methods

The study is divided into three stages and three different methods are used i.e. an analysis of students' written compositions, questionnaire and interview.

At the first and second stage, there were totally 113 participants (33 boys and 80 girls) involved in this study, from a senior high school in southern Taiwan. 42 students are from the first grade (i.e. freshmen), 32 students are from the second grade (i.e. juniors) and 39 students come from the third grade (i.e. seniors). For these participants English is a foreign language and a compulsory subject.

Writing a short English composition has been required since 1981 in the Joint University Entrance Examination. Although formal teaching in English writing is not introduced until the third year, those participants all have received the chance to practice writing no matter which grade they are in. Some of them have learnt English formally for 4 years (the freshman students), others 5 years (the junior students), and others 6 years (the senior students). However, what this study focuses on is not the number of errors made by different grades, but the frequency of error categories among different grades.

The first stage can be divided into 5 steps:

(1) Data collection: The procedure of collecting data in each class follows the same rule: students have to finish a short composition ranging from 80 to 120 words in forty minutes with the topics provided in classroom. Reference books, discussions, and explanations are prohibited during their writing. The whole procedure just simulated the Entrance Examination to be fair.

Five different types of topics are provided for writing and each student just chooses one topic interesting to him/her to write. They are the writing of a description *(School Sounds)*, a narration *(My Hometown, My Birthday Wish,* or *My Millennium Wish)*, a process *(How to Keep Your Girl-friend/ Boy-friend)*, a comparison and contrast *(Two Friends)*, and a cause and effect *(Are too Many People Going to College)*. The purpose of offering so many topics is to elicit as many different kinds of errors as possible. However, if students are not satisfied with any topic above, they can write what they are interested in.

After forty minutes, each student is required to submit his/her work no matter whether it is completed or not. There are almost 360 compositions collected totally at last. However, it is nearly impossible to correct all these 360 compositions; therefore, sampling is necessary. Here, all compositions within the same grade were mixed up and 25 compositions from each grade were selected randomly. Therefore, 75 compositions with different topics in total would be the samples in this study.

(2) Error checking: In order to reduce mis-correcting, I checked the compositions twice based on the following criteria:

- both global errors and local errors are corrected,
- content or meaning of the expression are kept intact,
- individual belief and cultural background to the topics are respected without any discriminations in the process of correcting,
- level of usage of the foreign language learners will be considered i.e. the style of written compositions should be formal (Chiang, 1993).

Although the correction of sampled compositions was solely conducted by me, yet a second checking was made to ensure there would be no any mistakes. In addition, the reliability of correction should be considered in light of the fact that I, as an English teacher who has been teaching English for many years in senior high school and university, have enough linguistic competence to correct those compositions. Besides, the words or expressions used by the senior high school students are not too difficult to deal with. Even if some usage is indeed beyond what I can comprehend, reference books and the colleagues are always ready for consulting.

(3) Classification of errors: To classify errors into categories may be the toughest task in error analysis because

one error may easily overlap with another. Unless a teacher discusses with students about the errors face to face, an error could not be categorised or interpreted easily. However, this difficulty should not discourage me from doing this research.

In this study, errors will be classified into three major groups: lexical, grammatical, and semantic categories for this categorisation can cater most writing errors made by Taiwanese students i.e. it is more contextualised. (Huang, 1988; Chiang, 1993; Lee, 1997)

All the errors in the study are classified into three main categories: (1) lexical errors, (2) grammatical errors, and (3) semantic (ill-formed) errors. The errors that do not belong to any of the above categories appropriately will be placed under the heading of "Miscellaneous Errors" (see Table 4). Under the heading of lexical errors are subcategories: spelling errors, compound errors, capitalisation errors, and morphology errors. The grammatical errors are put under the heads of verb errors, noun errors, pronoun errors, adverb errors, adjective errors, preposition errors, conjunction errors, interjection errors, determiner errors, punctuation errors, abbreviation errors, misplacement errors, violence of sentence structure, and violence of verb pattern. Tense errors, voice errors, mood errors, verbs with usage errors, infinitive errors, participle errors, gerund errors, S-V agreement errors, and auxiliary errors are included as the sub-subcategories under the head of verb errors.

Finally, semantic errors are grouped further into two subcategories: rhetoric errors and stylistic errors.

(4) Counting and registration of errors: Counting does play an important part in the process of data analysis because the method of it will dramatically influence the outcomes of the analysis and conclusions (Lee, 1997). Thus, how to enumerate should be treated deliberately. In this study, all these errors detected are counted on the basis of occurrence. Each occurrence will be enumerated as a single error. If a single error is made more than once, it will be counted more than once accordingly. However, if an error can be possibly classified into more than one category, only one occurrence will be adopted. Besides, every punctuation error is enumerated as a single error as well; however, when counting the grand total of words in the sampled compositions, punctuation is not included.

After the counting of all errors, the occurrences of all errors are registered in the error checklists. Each sampled composition is attached with an error checklist. At last, the total numbers of errors are summed up under each error category and then the percentage of each error type is calculated as well.

(5) Presentations of errors: In the next chapter, all categories of the errors made by the students will be discussed in detail. First of all, the overall description will include the tables of (1) the numbers of the total errors committed under each category in each grade, (2) the percentage of error

frequency under each category in each grade, (3) the total numbers and the percentages of simple or complex (including coordination and subordination sentences) sentences written in each grade, and (4) the frequencies of errors of per hundred words in the sampled compositions.

Finally, the general errors and some specific errors will be given explanations in the following section. The general errors can indicate the general writing problems most students may confront and thus can offer some pedagogical implications for English teachers to teach writing, while the specific errors can point out some students' special or unique writing problems. Briefly speaking, it is hoped the presentation of the errors could be helpful for students to notice some writing problems they may have and for teachers to understand why students commit such errors and then can adjust the teaching method to deal with those writing errors.

At the second stage, around one month latter, the same 113 participants were asked to complete a questionnaire. The questionnaire was constructed based on a mixed structure i.e. partly open questions and mostly closed questions. The purpose of conducting this questionnaire survey was to know if there are contextual factors that influence the learners' attitudes towards errors and error treatment. The original questionnaire was designed in Chinese. It was also translated into English for this book (see Appendix 3).

The questionnaire was piloted by two English teachers and 5 senior high school students (different from the participants) in Taiwan, and some revisions were made accordingly. After collecting all the questionnaires, I analysed the responses to each question, and calculated the percentage of each option in each question according to each group and the overall groups separately. Finally, the reasons why students chose their preferences were provided as well.

At the final stage, a group interview with 3 non-native English teachers of Taiwan was conducted. This took place as a group discussion rather than a traditional one-to-one style. Though the interview was also conducted in Taiwanese and Mandarin, an English transcript can be found in Appendix 6. The English transcript was checked by the interviewees to see if it represented their original ideas. The focus of the interview was on investigating teacher's opinions and reactions after knowing the results of the questionnaires done by the students. The findings from the second stage and the third stage will be discussed together in the latter section.

3.3 Limitations of the Study

Like all the previous research, inevitably there are some potential limitations existing in this study as well.

First of all, the generalisability in this study may not be convincing enough. The data were collected from only three senior high schools in Taiwan, whose ranking is placed in the middle among all senior high schools. In other words, those schools that rank either in the top or in the lowest are not considered in the study. Moreover, although different writing topics are provided for choosing, yet students are apt to choose the one which they are familiar with i.e. they would avoid the one they feel less confident in. In this way, it is very difficult to tell whether or not students have difficulties in operating some usage.

Besides, "there is not yet a universally valid norm of error frequency" (Chiang, 1993), therefore, if a standard norm of error frequency will be set up in the near future, the results of this study may be different from that. In addition, how to distinguish the competence error from the performance error is still a problem when a teacher is correcting students' compositions, which may slightly influence the result of the study. In this study, all errors identified are mainly deemed as competence errors.

Furthermore, the number of the participants is not large enough. All the participants are from the same senior high school. Hence, the results of the study may not be necessarily generalised to other high school students in Taiwan. Next, all the possible explanations of the results are the 'guesses' from teachers themselves. This may be different from what students really meant in original. Finally, some drawbacks of a questionnaire cannot be avoided in the study, either. It is difficult to know to what degree the participants' responses are reliable and true.

CHAPTER 4

FINDINGS, DISCUSSION, AND IMPLICATIONS

In this section, the findings and implications generated from the research will be presented and discussed. This part is divided into two main parts. Part A shows the findings from the first stage, and Part B includes the findings from the second and third stages.

4.1 Part A: The First Stage: Error Analysis

As discussed earlier, five topics requiring different writing styles were provided for students to choose from. As Table 1 shows, most students preferred to write the topic: My Hometown/ My Birthday Wish/ My Millennium Wish. These are all narrative writing. However, if we compare the students' preferences with the topics set by the Joint University Entrance Examination from 1986 to 2005 (see Appendix 4), near half of these topics are related to the writing of cause and effect (i.e. 9 out of 20.) Yet ironically enough, no narrative writing topic has appeared during the past 13 years.

Table 1:   The Percentage of Each Topic Chosen by the Students

Topics of Compositions	Freshman		Junior		Senior	
Description: School Sounds	0	0%	1	4%	1	4%
Narration: My Birthday Wish, My Home town, My Millennium Wish	18	72%	15	60%	11	44%
Process: How to Keep Your Girl/Boy Friend	0	0%	1	4%	1	4%
Comparison & Contrast: Two Friends	5	20%	5	20%	3	12%
Cause & Effect: Are Too Many People Going to College	2	8%	3	12%	2	8%
Others:	0	0%	0	0%	7	28%
Total:	25	100%	25	100%	25	100%

Secondly, in all the sentences collected, complex sentences (including subordination and coordination sentences) were used more frequently than simple sentences. This is the case in each grade. Table 2 shows that the percentages of the complex sentences and the simple ones are 58.09% and 41.9%.

Table 2: The Types of Sentences Written in the Compositions

	Freshman	*Junior*	*Senior*	*Total*
Sentences in Total	293	277	270	840
Simple Sentences	138	105	109	352
Percentage of Simple Sentences	*47.09%*	*37.90%*	*40.37%*	*41.90%*
Complex Sentences	155	172	161	488
Coordination	46	57	43	146
Subordination	109	115	118	342
Percentage of Complex Sentences	*52.90%*	*62.09%*	*59.62%*	*58.09%*

Moreover, as Table 2 indicates, subordination constructions were used more often then coordination ones. This result shows that senior high school students prefer to write complex sentences, especially subordination sentences. This does not necessarily mean that they have a good command of those constructions. A possible reason why the participants use complex constructions more frequently is that they believe that using complex sentences can make their compositions "look" more proficient. It might also be that students assume using those complex constructions can help them to obtain better grades. Good writers do need to be able to write complex sentences, but students can be advised to use simpler sentences.

Thirdly, a total of 9978 words was written in the 75 compositions, and 1206 errors were identified. This points out that 12.08 errors out of per hundred words were made by the students on average (see Table 3). Table 3 also shows that the senior group made the fewest mistakes and the freshmen group made the most.

Table 4 presents the frequencies of errors from the three groups, and percentages of the total error occurrences for each group.

Table 3: The Total Number of Words Written and Error Frequencies of per 100 Words

	Freshman	Junior	Senior	Total
Words in Total	2868	3064	4046	9978
Words in Average	114	122	161	132
Errors in Total	505	371	330	1206
Errors in per 100 words	17.60%	12.10%	8.10%	12.08%

Table 4: The Frequencies and Percentages of Errors in Each Category

Types of Errors	Freshman Freq. Pert.		Junior		Senior		Total	
Lexical Errors	**41**	**7.8%**	**51**	**13.5%**	**24**	**7.2%**	**116**	**9.5%**
Spelling Errors	27	5.3%	28	7.5%	15	4.5%	70	5.7%
Compound Errors	3	0.5%	7	1.8%	2	0.6%	12	0.5%
Capitalisation Errors	9	1.7%	12	3.2%	7	2.1%	28	2.3%
Morphology Errors	2	0.3%	4	1%	0	0%	6	0.4%
Grammatical Errors	**328**	**65.5%**	**216**	**58.6%**	**232**	**70.5%**	**776**	**64.8%**
Verb Errors	*77*	*14.5%*	*49*	*12.8%*	*63*	*18.5%*	*189*	*15.2%*
Tense Errors	27	5.3%	15	4%	22	7.2%	64	5.5%
Voice Errors	4	0.7%	3	0.8%	1	0.3%	8	0.6%
Mood Errors	3	0.5%	1	0.2%	5	1.5%	9	0.7%
Error Usage of Verb	16	3.1%	12	3.2%	15	4.5%	43	3.6%
Infinitive Errors	1	0.1%	0	0%	8	2.4%	9	0.8%
Participles Errors	3	0.5%	4	1%	6	1.8%	13	1.1%
Gerund Errors	5	0.9%	1	0.2%	0	0%	6	0.3%
S-V agreement Errors	8	1.5%	7	1.8%	2	0.6%	17	1.3%
Auxiliary Errors	10	1.9%	6	1.6%	4	1.2%	20	1.5%
Noun Errors	*61*	*11.8%*	*33*	*8.7%*	*52*	*15.6%*	*146*	*12%*
Number & Countability	30	5.9%	18	4.8%	25	7.5%	73	6%
Case Errors	7	1.3%	2	0.5%	2	0.6%	11	0.8%
Gender Errors	0	0%	0	0%	2	0.6%	2	0.2%
Error Usage of Noun	15	2.9%	5	1.3%	15	4.5%	35	2.9%

	Freq	Pert	Freq	Pert	Freq	Pert	Freq	Pert
Pronoun Errors	9	1.7%	8	2.1%	8	2.4%	25	2%
Adverb Errors	14	2.7%	12	3.2%	12	4.6%	38	3.1%
Adjective Errors	19	3.7%	24	6.4%	22	6.6%	65	5.5%
Preposition Errors	22	4.3%	8	2.1%	24	7.2%	54	4.5%
Conjunction Errors	62	12.2%	29	7.8%	5	1.5%	96	7.1%
Interjection Errors	0	0%	0	0%	0	0%	0	0%
Determiner Errors	11	2.1%	17	4.5%	19	5.7%	47	4.1%
Punctuation Errors	18	3.5%	8	2.1%	4	1.2%	30	2.2%
Abbreviation Errors	1	0.1%	2	0.5%	10	3%	13	1.2%
Misplacement Errors	8	1.5%	8	2.1%	5	1.5%	21	1.7%
Violation of Sentence	28	5.5%	20	5.3%	11	3.3%	59	4.7%
Violation of Verb Pattern	7	1.3%	6	1.6%	5	1.5%	18	1.4%
Semantic Errors	**129**	**25.4%**	**101**	**27.1%**	**74**	**22.3%**	**304**	**24.9%**
Rhetoric Errors	54	10.6%	60	16.1%	46	13.9%	160	13.5%
Stylistic Errors	75	14.8%	41	11%	28	8.4%	144	11.4%
Miscellaneous Errors	**7**	**1.3%**	**3**	**0.8%**	**0**	**0%**	**10**	**0.7%**
Total	**505**	**100%**	**371**	**100%**	**330**	**100%**	**1206**	**100%**

N.B. Freq: Frequency, Pert: Percentage

In these following sections, we would like to discuss what the statistics above imply in details.

4.1.1 Lexical errors

A total of 116 occurrences of errors, equal to 9.5%, is identified as the lexical errors in the sample compositions, including (1) spelling errors, (2) compound errors, (3) capitalisation errors, and (4) morphology errors. The following Table 5 and Figure 1 describe the statistics of overall lexical errors and the hierarchy of lexical errors respectively.

Table 5: The Frequencies of Lexical Errors

Types of Errors	Freshman (%)	Junior (%)	Senior (%)	Average (%)
Lexical Errors	**41, 7.8%**	**51, 13.5%**	**24, 7.2%**	**116, 9.5%**
Spelling Errors	27, 5.3%	28, 7.5%	15, 4.5%	70, 5.7%
Compound Errors	3, 0.5%	7, 1.8%	2, 0.6%	12, 0.5%
Capitalization Errors	9, 1.7%	12, 3.2%	7, 2.1%	28, 2.3%
Morphology Errors	2, 0.3%	4, 1%	0, 0%	6, 0.4%

Figure 1: The Hierarchy of Spelling Errors

Spelling errors (70, 5.7%)

1

Capitalisation errors (28, 2.3%)

1

Compound errors (12, 0.5%)

1

Morphology errors (6, 0.4%)

4.1.1.1 Spelling errors

Of the 116 lexical errors, 70 (5.7%) errors are misspelled by the subjects, and in each group spelling errors also occur most frequently compared with the other categories (27, 5.3% in the freshman group; 28, 7.5% in the junior group; 15, 4.5% in the senior group). Interestingly, on the average the junior students commit more spelling errors then the freshman students. However, this outcome does not imply that the freshman students completely have a higher command of English spelling than the junior students do. The possible reasons may be that firstly the freshman group only uses very easy vocabulary they already know and secondly since the junior group has acquired more vocabulary and thus are more willingly to risk spelling new words.

It is clearly obvious that misspelling may not come from the mother tongue interference because Chinese and English have two thoroughly different writing systems. All we can conclude is that it should be the students' incomplete learning causing errors.

Generally speaking, the possible reasons are: (1) Inaccurate pronunciation e.g. 21*clup (club), 46* rever (river), *43 visiters (visitors), and 53* Contantly (Constantly), which implies that students are still unable to distinguish most English minimal pairs; besides, due to the silent sound of the final '–e' in English, the students would always omit the final '-e' while spelling, such as 9* celebrat (celebrate).

(2) Unfamiliarity: this means that students are not familiar with the words they will spell but rather try to spell them at risk by applying similarly-looking words, for example 31*opinios (opinions), 21* civitizens (citizens), 5* presurved (preserved), and 42* industral (industrial).

(3) Chance misspelling: some misspelled words do not mean the students have no idea of how to spell words but rather occur by chance. 1* is order to (in order to), 6* Aand (And), and 60* two many (too many) are instances. It seems that the freshman group has more chances in misspelling a word accidentally. These mistakes could be corrected by students themselves if they have been warned to pay attention to vocabulary-checking after their writing.

In sum, misspelling errors occur quite often among English learners in the process of writing and to prevent these errors, students should be given direct remedial instructions and be encouraged to look up unfamiliar words in the dictionary more often once confronting new vocabulary. Therefore, this has implications for dictionary training.

4.1.1.2 Compound errors

Compound words refer to those that are formed by combining two different words. They are written in the form of two separate words or a single word with a hyphen. In this study, the subjects commit far less compound errors than the previous category. A total of 12 errors (0.5%) is made, including 3 (0,5%) from the freshman group, 7 (1.8%) from the junior group, and 2 (0.6%) from the senior group. More interestingly again, the freshman group has a lower error frequency in this category compared with the other two groups. Similarly, the reason why very few compound words are used by the freshman group is that the students have less confidence or less linguistic competence (i.e. not knowing too many compound words) in operating compound words and thus avoid using them. Some compound errors made in the study are like 6* boyfriend (boy-friend/ boy friend), 14* girlfriend (girl-friend/ girl friend), and 64* someplace (some place). As discussed previously, the best way to avoid this error is to look up a dictionary to check the correct forms.

4.1.1.3 Capitalisation error

A total of 28 capitalisation errors (2.3%) is identified in the study. The error occurrences and frequencies in each group are 9 (1.7%) in the freshman group, 12 (3.2%) in the junior group, and 7 (2.1%) in the senior group. The outcomes may imply that the subjects are too careless to avoid those errors. Clearly, there seems no capitalisation rule in Chinese writing, and without doubt there is no room for mother tongue negative transfer.

However, the occurrences and frequencies are a little higher than expected. Maybe most English teachers suppose students should have had a clear idea of how and when to capitalise an English word and thus ignore the capitalisation problems students may meet. Examples of this are 2*...buy a Bass (...buy a bass), 3* ...Kaohsiung, Which... (...Kaohsiung, which...), 36* I think Whether ... (I think whether...), 49* ...many people going to College. (...many people going to college.), 53* during this time,... (During this time,...), and 59* ...the international airport is not far... (...the International Airport is not far...). Some learners tend to easily capitalise a word after a comma or do not know to capitalise a proper noun. These errors could be avoided through teachers' instructions and students' checking.

4.1.1.4 Morphology errors

Morphological errors here refer to the meanings or the functions of the morpheme the students misuse or misunderstand. For example, the indefinite articles (a and an) should be applied accurately according to the first sound of the following sound e.g. a pen, a book, but an apple. In the study, only a total of 6 (0.4%) morphological errors committed by the subjects, which has the fewest occurrences in the lexical errors. No such error is made by the senior group but the freshman group make 2 errors (0.3%) of it and the junior group make 4 errors (1.0%). However, there is an interesting case here i.e. in the junior group 3 out of 4 error occurrences come solely from the same subject and obviously this students should be given special remedial teaching to cure this problem.

7* …every senior high school students' hope. (…every senior high school student's hope.), 21* a exam (an exam), 40* a interesting… (an interesting…), and 45* dogs's (dogs'), birds's (birds'), students's (students') are example of this. The main reason why the students commit this error is probably because they over-generalise some grammatical rule and thus do not take notice of its restriction.

In brief, it can be observed form the above discussion that in the lack of confidence the students may try to avoid using the words they are not familiar with and thus make the error frequencies of the lexical category is fewer than other main categories. However, if the students do commit lexical errors, the reasons are mainly from their learning problems e.g. simplify or over-generalise grammatical rules due to the lack of complete linguistic competence. What students can do is study harder and perhaps teachers would like to adjust the strategies of teaching vocabulary as well.

4.1.2 Grammatical errors

In this study, grammatical errors refer to the unacceptable expressions or usage in the scope of grammar rules in English.

In other words, the subjects would commit such a grammatical error if he/she does not follow the rules of grammar correctly. Of all the 1206 errors in the study, 776 of them are grammatical errors. It takes up to 64.8% of the overall errors. Obviously, the subjects in three groups all have great difficulties in operating grammatical rules right. The proportions of grammatical errors in each group all rank the highest: 328 errors (65.5%) in the freshman group, 216 errors (58.6%) in the junior group, and 232 errors (70.5%) in the senior group.

Very surprisingly, although the freshman group commits more grammatical errors than the other two groups, yet the proportion of grammatical errors in the senior group ranks the highest among the three groups. It implies that the longer one learns, not necessarily the less grammatical problems he/she might have. This may be because the students in the senior group would prefer to apply more difficult or complex constructions than the other groups and thus they have more chances committing errors. The frequencies of using complex sentences can explain this (see Table. 2). Does the mother tongue really interfere the acquisition of grammatical rules or simply students have poor learning strategies toward English learning? This puzzle indeed needs to be noticed by English teachers in the process of teaching writing.

4.1.2.1 Verb errors

There is no denying that a verb plays a very essential and important role in an English sentence. However, a verb may contain various forms and usage; as a result of this, it is natural that students would misuse them and commit errors. The statistics of this study also shows that verb errors in each group possess the highest proportions than other subcategories of the grammatical errors. A total of 189 verb errors (15.2%) in the study is made by the subjects and respectively the freshman students enjoy 77 errors (14.5%) among the overall errors of this group, the junior group commit 49 errors (12.8%), and 63 errors (15.2%) are from the senior group. The following Table 6 and Figure 2 show the total verb errors and the hierarchy of verb errors.

Table 6: The Frequencies of Verb Errors

Types of Errors	Freshman (%)	Junior (%)	Senior (%)	Average (%)
Verb Errors	*77, 14.5%*	*49, 12.8%*	*63, 18.5%*	*189, 15.2%*
Tense Errors	27, 5.3%	15, 4%	22, 7.2%	64, 5.5%
Voice Errors	4, 0.7%	3, 0.8%	1, 0.3%	8, 0.6%
Mood Errors	3, 0.5%	1, 0.2%	5, 1.5%	9, 0.7%
Error Usage of Verb	16, 3.1%	12, 3.2%	15, 4.5%	43, 3.6%
Infinitive Errors	1, 0.1%	0, 0%	8, 2.4%	9, 0.8%

Participles Errors	3, 0.5%	4, 1%	6, 1.8%	13, 1.1%
Gerund Errors	5, 0.9%	1, 0.2%	0, 0%	6, 0.3%
S-V agreement Errors	8, 1.5%	7, 1.8%	2, 0.6%	17, 1.3%
Auxiliary Errors	10, 1.9%	6, 1.6%	4, 1.2%	20, 1.5%

Figure 2: The Hierarchy of Verb Errors

Tense errors (64, 5.5%)

    ↓

Error usage of verbs (43, 3.6%)

    ↓

Auxiliary errors (20, 1.5%)

    ↓

S-V agreement errors (17, 1.3%)

    ↓

Participle errors (13, 1.1%)

    ↓

Infinitive errors (9, 0.8%)

    ↓

Mood errors (9, 0.7%)

    ↓

Voice errors (8, 0.6%)

    ↓

Gerund errors (6, 0.3%)

4.1.2.2 Tense errors

Statistically speaking, tense error is the largest group in the verb error category. As what discussed in the preceding parts, there are too many various forms in verbs and so are verb tenses in English. Roughly speaking, there are six tenses in total in English and misuse of a verb tense would damage the meaning undoubtedly e.g. "I will go to see a movie." is absolutely different from the meaning of the sentence "I went to see a movie." Thus, a sentence like "I would have done it tomorrow morning." should be treated right away for an error involving the misuse of tense is a global error, which would, with no doubt, cause the breakdown of communication in English writing. Here are some examples of tense errors from the sample compositions.

8*   When I am in junior high school, I have two friends. (When I was in junior high school, I had …)

9*   My birthday was in 11.10. (My birthday is …)

10* I was born there, and lived for eleven years. (I was born there and had lived there for 11 years.)

15* My home town was far away the big city because this factor makes it quiet. (My home town is far away the big city, …)

18* And if it happened, that will hurt you. (… it happens, that will hurt you.)

33* …they will talk to others friendly when we are visited there.

(…they will…when we visit…)

46* At that time, I often fish and carry fish… (…, I often fished and carried…)

55* We were young, pretty… (We are young…)

61* On that day, I as usual make three… (…, I as usual made three…)

63* So if you felt your life was so boring,… (So if you feel…is so boring,…)

From the above examples and others in the sample compositions, we can find that the subjects tend to use the past tense instead of the present tense. One simple reason can be given as follows: the subjects misunderstand the complex English system. Furthermore, students' incomplete linguistic competence and over-correction may account for the occurrences as well. When teaching verb tense, English teachers should clearly specify under which situation is a peculiar verb tense used. Examples using the same context with different verb tenses may be useful for students to distinguish verb tenses e.g.:

I had lived in Kaohsiung for 10 years.

I have lived in Kaohsiung for 10 years.

I live in Kaohsiung now.

I will have lived in Kaohsiung for 10 years by the end of this June.

Another possible reason may be from the mother tongue

interference, "since in Chinese, the syntactic tense device is less important in indicating time sequence" (Huang, 1988: 43). In Chinese, there is no verb tense existing and thus time sequence is distinguished by time adverbial. For example,

我 (wo)　明天 (ming-tien)　要看電影 (yao-kan-dein-yin)

I　　　　tomorrow　　　　will go to see a movie.

我 (wo) 昨天 (zuo-tien) 看了一場電影 (kan-le-I-chang-dein-yin)

I　　　yesterday　　　went to see a movie.

Therefore, it can be assumed that the students who would make such errors may think in the first language and then translate the ideas into the foreign language.

4.1.2.3 Voice errors and Mood errors

In the study, examples of the voice errors are like these:

2* …most of them can't be come true… (…can't come true…)

40* We three are known... (We three know…)

63* …will not be come true… (…will not come true…)

Generally speaking, the subjects have fewer difficulties in using active voice and passive voice (see Table 6). However, in the sampled compositions, most sentences are written in active voice. The students, using active voice more frequently, may know that sentences with active voice are easier, more direct, and economical than sentence with passive voice. However, it is worth bearing in mind that students may also avoid using passive voice because of less confidence and competence. This can be detected by giving them some exercise with passive voice.

Similarly, mood errors are made less by the subjects. Only 9 errors are found in the study, which constitutes 0.7% in the grand errors. Although the senior group enjoys higher error frequency (1.5%) than the other two groups (0.5%, 0.2% respectively), yet the errors mainly come from the same subject. Examples are

20* I wish I can design many kinds of clothes. (I wish I could...)
26* If I have a motorcycle, I wouldn't be... (If I had a motorcycle, I wouldn't...)

The result indicates that the subjects would easily get confused with subjunctive mood. This may be due to their incomplete learning or interference from mother tongue. In Chinese, a sentence with subjunctive mood will simply be accompanied with 如果 ru-guo (if), no change with verbs is compulsory.

4.1.2.4 Error usage of verb, Infinite errors, Participles errors, and Gerund errors

A total of 43 errors is related to error usage of verb, which constitutes 3.6% of the grand error. Again, the error frequency in the senior group (4.5%) is a little bit higher than the other groups. (3.1% and 3.2%). We many assume that there must be some reasons making the senior students commit more errors than other groups. First, the senior students may tend to use difficult verbs easily regardless of the usage restrictions. Second, the interference from Chinese does always exist with the time of learning. The students would use translation method in writing English compositions, which makes their Chinese-laden sentences quite odd. Finally, most of them are still poor in collocation due to their incomplete knowledge. Below are some examples of this area.

7* I hope my parents can take much money. (…earn much money.)

12* She just over her senior high school class. (…just completed/finished…)

33* You shouldn't limit what he wants to do. (…prohibit what…)

46* …that it will return the country I used to be. (…will become…)

52* I can join a good university. (…attend a …)

53* At class, we speak these lessons. (…read these lessons.)

55* Angela likes…look at books. (…read books.)

As to the infinite form errors (infinitive, participle and gerund), a total of 28 errors is found, which constitutes 4.4% of the grand errors. In each group, the freshman group commits 9 errors (1.5%); the junior group, 5 errors (1.2%), and 14 errors (4.2%) in the senior group. It seems that the senior high students should be hinted at avoiding using the complex constructions they are not familiar with. Too much risk-taking results in more errors. Examples of this area are like these.

4* I need to found… (I need to find…)

11* People lives there are friendly.   (People living there…)

17* …many wishes, like buy… (…, like buying…)

28* Standing alone in the forest, the water… (My standing alone…, the water…)

67* …it would to be… (… it would be…)

69* I start believe… (I start to believe…)

75* My jobs are not so many but study.   (…but to study.)

Generally speaking, the infinitive marker "to" is a problem for the subjects. The subjects may inappropriately or incorrectly omit "to", which may be due to the transfer from the mother tongue. In Chinese, two bare verbs can be placed together without any problem e.g. 我喜歡看書 wo-shi-huan-kan-su (I like read books). Thus such error would appear quite often in

Taiwanese students' writings. Moreover, the misuse of "to" may be an induced error as well. Some English teachers would teach students that "use a bare verb after 'to'"; therefore, an expression like "look forward to see you soon" would possibly be made. With regard to the gerund and participles errors, they are mainly from intralinguistic interference i.e. the grammatical rules of forming a participle or a gerund are not learnt well and thus are misused.

4.1.2.5 S-V agreement errors and Auxiliary errors

The problems of S-V agreement errors could be easily prevented once students can check carefully each subject and verb to see if they agree closely. So, there are implications here for training students to check their work thoroughly. A total of 17 errors are found, which constitutes 1.3% of the grand total. Examples identified are like these.

16* Penny is a…and treat everyone… (…treats everyone…)

17* God say… (God says…)

44* I love my hometown where have blue sky.   (…,which has blue sky…)

48* …friends is good for… (…are good…)

52* That are my birthday wish. (…is my…)

64* It is a home that make… (…that makes…)

Although Huang (1988: 55) asserts that "in Chinese there is no auxiliary verbs that function like those in English, so students often fail to acquire them correctly", yet in this study, we can see that with time of learning, the subjects commit less and less auxiliary errors (1.9%, 1.6%, 1.2% respectively). Therefore, it may be assumed that these auxiliary errors are mainly due to intralinguistic interference and can be avoided by acquiring more accurate grammar rules. A total of 20 errors is found in this area, which makes up 1.5% of the grand total. Here are some examples.

11* It rains not very much. (…does not rain…)

17* …we don't have a lot of wishes. (…should not have…)

20* I don't tell anybody until my dream… (I will not…until…)

36* …so you don't worry you will lose him. (…you have not to worry…)

40* I still want not to… (…do not want to…)

47* You take actions and not give up. (…and do not give up.)

63* Why I have so many dreams? (Why do I…?)

71* …he yet come home. (…he did not come home yet.)

A suggestion for the subjects is to notice the modals for one's willingness such as can, have to, should, or will, and auxiliaries in the negative sentences.

4.1.2.6 Noun Errors

Of the total errors, 146 errors belong to noun errors, which constitutes 12.0% of the grand total. Although the frequency of noun errors is less than that of verb errors, which may imply that the students do not have too many problems in this area, yet the senior group still enjoys the highest error frequency of all error occurrences (15.6%) compared with the other two groups. In fact, a golden rule of writing -- correctness is far more important than complexity - - should be instructed to the senior students clearly. The hierarchy of difficulty of this area is illustrated in Figure 3, and Table 7 shows the error frequencies of the noun category.

Table 7: The Frequencies of Noun Errors

Types of Errors	Freshman (%)	Junior (%)	Senior (%)	Average (%)
Noun Errors	*61, 11.8%*	*33, 8.7%*	*52, 15.6%*	*146, 12%*
Number & Countability	30, 5.9%	18, 4.8%	25, 7.5%	73, 6%
Case Errors	7, 1.3%	2, 0.5%	2, 0.6%	11, 0.8%
Gender Errors	0. 0%	0, 0%	2, 0.6%	2, 0.2%
Error Usage of Noun	15, 2.9%	5, 1.3%	15, 4.5%	35, 2.9%
Pronoun Errors	9, 1.7%	8, 2.1%	8, 2.4%	25, 2%

Figure 3: The Hierarchy of Noun Errors

Number & Countability (73, 9.9%)

1

Pronoun Errors (25, 2.0%)

1

Error Usage of Noun (35, 2.9%)

1

Case Error (11, 0.8%)

1

Gender Error (2, 0.2%)

4.1.2.7 Number and Conutability

A number error means the misuse of the singular form for the plurals form or vice versa. A total of 73 errors is identified in the study, which takes up 6.0% of the grand total. Again, the senior group has a higher error frequency (7.5%) in this error category than the other groups (5.9% in the freshman group; 6.6% in the junior group).   Quite a few examples of number errors are as follows:

3*   …more information than other city.   (…than other cities.)

6*   …all the wish… (…all the wishes…)

8*   My best friend, Amy and July,… (My best friends, Amy and July,…)

13* Do you have any wishes?   (…any wish?)

17* …all kind of bags… (…all kinds of bags…)

18* I think friend who is a … (I think a friend who is a…)

20* I make effort… (I make efforts…)

42* …many environment threat… (…many environmental threats…)

45* …many interesting different thing… (…many different interesting things…)

46* There are many farmer… (…many farmers…)

48* I full of thank… (…full of thanks…)

51* Here is country. (…a country.)

52* I'm the third year senior high school students. (…student.)

55* Another good friends of mine is… (Another good friend of…)

57* I have two friend… (I have two friends…)

58* It's not like general cities. (…a general city.)

67* It's not a good places. (…a good place.)

From the above examples, it can be concluded that the errors mainly fall into three types: (1) the use of the singular instead of the plural or vice versa, (2) the most noticeable one, the number of the noun clashes with a number adjective like "many", and (3) the misuse of the pattern "one of Ns". The possible reasons may be due to that telling a countable noun from an uncountable noun in English is slightly difficult for Taiwanese students owing to the different views in countability toward nouns between two different cultures. For example, it is very hard to make a Taiwanese student believe 'rice' is an uncountable noun in English. Secondly, it may result from the students' inability to recognise collective nouns or irregular nouns in English, and finally "slip of pen" (carelessness) may be another reason to account for this error.

4.1.2.8 Case errors and Gender errors

A total of 11 case errors is found in the study, which constitutes 0.8% of the grand total. From the Table 7, we can find that the freshman group has more difficulty in this area because they enjoy a higher error frequency (1.3%) than the other two groups. Generally speaking, the cases of a pronoun would cause more problems than a noun since the three cases of a noun is nearly the same. The following examples can support this assertion.

5*   …Taiwan's culture… (…Taiwanese culture…)

6*   …my parents will let my go to… (…will let me go…)

9*   …my friends and me wouldn't … (…my friends and I wouldn't…)

11* It makes we must to wear… (It makes us to…)

50* …yet both of they are… (…both of them are…)

55* …she is more quiet than us. (… quieter than we.)

74* …he is smarter then me. (…smarter than I.)

The possible reason may rely on that students would use the translation method in the process of writing English compositions. Since there is no big difference in the forms of three cases of pronouns in Chinese, the students would naturally commit errors like these. However, in comparative sentences, students would tend to use the objective case more often than the nominative, which usually causes ambiguity for correctors. One typical example is *40 ...he treats friends better than me. Unless the teacher knows exactly what the student tries to convey, it is easily to misunderstand the meaning of such sentence.

In this study, only two gender errors are found in the senior group from the subject, which constitute 0.2% of the grand total. For example,

*62 On the other hand, the man who has got into college... (On the other hand, the people who...)

Strictly speaking, it is not that the subject has no idea of gender in writing but s/he misuses the "man" to refer to both man and woman in his/her writing, which is seldom acceptable nowadays. To sum up, the students seem to have no problem with gender errors; however, a correct gender term should be always chosen appropriately and carefully in a good writing.

4.1.2.9 Error usage of noun

Here, an error usage of noun means the misuse of a noun for another. The subjects may choose a wrong noun to represent their idea due to the direct translation from the mother tongue or inability to notice the collocational nature. Most Taiwanese students would think there are always two equivalent words existing in both English and Chinese due to the influence of using a monolingual English-Chinese dictionary. Therefore, they would easily misuse some nouns that are not understood by native speakers but by their English teachers only. A total of 35 errors are identified in the study, which constitutes 2.9% of the grand total. Again, risk-taking makes the senior students commit more errors (4.5%) than the other two groups (2.9% in the freshman group; 1.3% in the junior group). The followings are some examples of this error category.

16* They are different in some places. (…in some aspects.)

20* …design many kinds of clothes… (…different styles of …)

22* They can talk about their future,…their mind. (…, their secrets.)

25* In my mind, to be a good worker is… (In my viewpoint,…)

38* Tainan is a traditional place in structures. (…in buildings.)

46* …it (hometown) became the different face. (…a different view.)

52* I have several dreams and some purposes. (…and some

targets.)

53* I find it exciting to make friendship. (…make friends.)

55* …the word, "to win out, we must first…" (…the saying,…)

62* The amount of people who… (The number of people…)

63* …they are the target to keep me going. (...are the power to keep…)

The above examples tell us that to write a good composition, direct translation from the mother tongue should be avoided, especially for the language learners in Taiwan.

4.1.2.10 Pronoun errors

Keeping writing without referring to the previous is not a good writing method. A total of 25 errors is categorised as pronoun errors, which constitutes 2.0% of the grand total. The senior group, again, enjoys the higher error frequency (2.4%) than the other groups. Usually the subjects would use pronouns like 'this', 'that', or 'it' to refer to something he/she has already known. However, due to the careless application, readers would easily get confused with these pronouns. To avoid intriguing any misunderstanding, careful checks of the used pronouns should be executed after writing. Here are some examples.

4* I always tell me one thing. (…myself one thing.)

17* They will say we should work hard and they will come true. (…and dreams will come true.)

22* The other one must hope that she can trust each other. (no suggestion)

22* There are two elementary schools which I had… (…schools where…)

25* The first one, they built many colleges… (…, the government built…)

27* I thought if you work harder, then wishes… (…if I work…)

28* …became a dream where I could never… (… a dream which…)

30* If I were him, we wouldn't… (If I were him, I wouldn't…)

44* I love my hometown where have… (…my hometown which…)

53* The month of July in which it would change… (…of July would change…)

55* We have the same desire which is… (…desire that is…)

56* Many friends around me encourage me to study in the library, where is quieter. (…,because it is quieter.)

57* I have two friends, one is Mary, another is… (…one is…and the other is…)

65* If a student would like to be more familiar with other students, it's really not the only way. (no suggestion).

From the above examples, we can find that students do not know how to match a pronoun with the mentioned noun correctly and quite evidently the higher grade one is, the more possibly he/she will commit the relative pronoun errors. However, this does not mean the freshman group has no problem of this but simply due to that the freshman students have not learnt the relative pronouns so far yet. "Prevention is better than cure." English teachers should pay attention to this phenomenon deliberately.

4.1.2.11 Adverb errors and Adjective errors

In English, adverbs and adjectives share the same function; besides, their meaning and forms are quite similar. Thus the subjects would misuse them quite easily. In this study, a total of 38 errors are adverb errors, constituting 3.1% of the grand total, while 65 errors are identified as adverb errors, which takes up 5.5% of the grand total. Obviously, the subjects have more difficulties in using adjectives than in using adverbs. Examples of these errors are as follows.

1* I believe I can be success. (…can be successful.)

2* It is more easy to… (…easier to…)

3* …much cars… (…many cars…)

4* I can study more harder. (…study harder.)

6* …be happy and health every day. (…and healthy…)

19* It is noise, busy and… (…noisy…)

30* …who study very harder… (…much harder…)

31* …lets we feel we very cool and inquired. (no suggestion)

32* …wants her things to keep cleaning. (…clean.)

38* … in south Taiwan… (in southern Taiwan…)

52* I hope they can live happy and … (…live happily…)

53* It's a little rounded world… (…round world…)

67* It's not crowd. (…crowded.)

To sum up, in operating adverbs or adjectives students may (1) misspell the desired words, (2) use an adverb instead of an adjective and vice versa, (3) have no idea of the difference between 'much' and 'very', (4) use nouns to replace adjectives, (5) use double comparatives, and (6) wrongly suppose all verbs ended with '-ing' or '-ed' could be used as adjectives. The main reason may come from students' inadequate linguistic competence i.e. over-generalising or simplifying the usage of adjectives and adverbs.

4.1.2.12 Prepositions errors, Conjunction errors and Interjection errors

In English, prepositions are applied according to idioms and usage rather than grammar rules. Thus, most Taiwanese students would be required to learn the prepositions by heart. However, due to their incomplete learning and interference from Chinese, preposition errors are still easily committed. In Chinese, 'in', 'on', or 'at' all can be translated as "zai 在". Therefore, when students cannot find an equivalence in their mother tongue, they would choose randomly or omit a preposition. In the study, a total of 54 preposition errors are found, which constitutes 4.5% of the grand total. Compared with other error categories, the error frequency is a little bit higher, which shows the subjects are still not confident in using prepositions. Moreover, the senior group seems to have great difficulties in applying prepositions; the error frequency is 7.2% in this group but this cannot be interpreted that the freshman and junior groups have less problems in using preposition for they may use avoidance strategy. The followings show some examples of preposition errors.

1*　go to the college about art (…art college)

4*　in my every birthday (on my birthday)

5*　I was born in here. (I was born here.)

9*　my birthday is in 11.20. (my birthday is on…)

14*　My birthday will be coming up. (…coming soon.)

15*　far away the city (far away from the city)

24*　in the night (at night)

28*　the forest nearby a lake (…near a lake)

30*　..limited in many… (…limited to…)

45*　When you go along in classroom… (go along with the classroom…)

55*　…be ready to J.C.E.E. (…be ready for the…)

60*　They are involved on… (…involved in…)

68*　…many the youth of our country. (…in our country.)

75*　…the same with the passed years. (…the same as the past years.)

In conjunction errors, a total of 96 errors is identified in the study, which constitutes 7.1% of the grand total. Among all error categories, conjunction errors rank the second highest, which implies the subjects have more difficulties in operating conjunctions appropriately. Generally speaking, the freshman group commits quite a few conjunction errors (62, 12.2%), compared with the junior group (29, 7.8%) and the senior group (5, 1.5%); however, perhaps we can foresee that the conjunction errors will occur less and less with the student's learning during the following academic years. Therefore, first of all, we may say intralinguistic interference is one of the reasons causing conjunction problems.

The following examples can roughly grouped into three categories: (1) double conjunctions, (2) improper conjunctions, and (3) the omission of conjunctions.

3*   But I still like Taipei. (However, I still like Taipei.)

4*   I can study more harder now than previously, don't fish in the troubled water. (…, and should not…)

6*   And I also want to have a boyfriend. (Besides,…)

8*   But she doesn't like boys. (However, …)

10* When I graduate from college, I will… (After I…)

16* But we can work hard to change the mistake together. (However,…)

21* …going to college is helpful for us when we will want to find a job… (…if we…)

27* I hope that the world is peaceful, everybody will wish… (…and everybody…)

29* She is thin and her face is very long… (…but her face…)

32* Lisa is very smart, quiet, careful person. (…,and careful person.)

36* You shouldn't lie to him and love him. (…but love him.)

50* Much as them have not interests in common, yet both… (…, but both…)

54* And then, I have a wonderful in the college. (Then,…)

55* And I often sing, play basketball, shopping. (Besides,…, and go shopping.)

57* Because I was a shy boy, and I studies… (I was…, and…)

61* And the final wish, I thought it… (As to the …)

70* And it's bad than writing. (Moreover, it's…)

73* And I can relax and do what I want to do. (Then…and…)

74* In addition, he likes to play computer games and I am not interested in using … (In addition,…but I am not…)

From the above examples, we can find that the subjects seem to use 'and' quite often, especially in the beginning of a sentence. This may be due to the mother tongue interference partially for there is no limitation in using conjunctions among sentences in Chinese. Moreover, owing to their inadequate knowledge about the relationships between coordination or subordination clauses, choosing the wrong conjunction would occur easily.

Besides, although there are few correlative conjunction errors found in the sample compositions, yet in fact, Taiwanese students are still not very sure about the correct usage like 'not only...but also...', '...so...that...', or '...neither...nor...', especially 'Unless...or...', 'Because...so...', and 'Although...but...' are misused quite often. For example, 32* Although they have different characters, but they... (Although...,they...). That is because students translate their ideas directly from Chinese into English. The above wrong collocations are totally acceptable in Chinese, so the subjects would commit such errors naturally when writing English compositions. To sum up, due to incomplete L2 linguistic competence, insufficient confidence, and partial L1 interference, the subjects commit such conjunction errors.

Not surprisingly at all, there are no interjection errors in the sample compositions. However, it does not mean the subjects will never commit this error and have no difficulty in applying interjections. In this study, no interjection is applied and thus the reasons of making such error cannot be predicted exactly. However, we may, in fact, suppose the reason why there is no interjection used in the sample compositions. That is the influence of traditional culture. In a traditional society, students are taught to depress their rich emotions implicitly in writing rather than expressing them out vividly or wildly. All what they can do is rightly write without strong emotional expressions such as using interjections.

4.1.2.13 Determiner errors

Learning English determiners always seems to be an enigma for non-native speakers, especially those with no article system in their language like Chinese. However, it is a pity that the attitude of many non-native English learners and some English teachers toward English articles is that articles are redundant in English and have no effect on communication. In fact, although articles are so-called function words in English, yet the misuse of them would sometimes cause serious misunderstanding and certainly, repeated article errors can be irritating to a reader and create a bad impression. In addition, articles in English have the semantic functions of determination and demonstration as well; therefore, they indeed need special attention while writing.

In the study, a total of 47 determiner errors is found, constituting 4.1% of the grand total. The freshman subjects commit 11 errors (2.1%), the junior students have 17 errors (4.5%), and 19 errors (5.7%) are found in the senior group. Determiner errors will be divided into four groups as follows (Yin, 1996).

4.1.2.14 Co-occurrence

This means the juxtaposition of articles with deictic words.
16* ...my the best friends... (...my best friend...)
56* ...my this year's birthday wish... (...my birthday wish this

year…)

The reasons why learners make such errors might be that firstly, at an early stage of learning English, the subjects are apt to have a holistic learning set of the target language; therefore, they operate nominals as an undifferentiated class in which the articles are not discriminated from other determiners. Secondly, it may result from the interference of mother tongue. In English, any common noun must be preceded by one and only one determiner, but there is no such rule in Chinese.

4.1.2.15 Underextension

This refers to the omission of determiners.

10* In downtown, there… (In the downtown, …)

26* I go to bus stop… (…the bus stop…)

27* …know that college exam plays… (…the college exam…)

35* …in future… (…in the future…)

45* …, and Teacher is anger… (…,and our teacher is angry…)

48* First one is that… (The first one…)

53* …be ready for J.C.E.E… (…be ready for the J.C.E.E…)

Possible reasons to account for the errors are first of all, the subjects apply the strategies of simplification and avoidance while learning English, especially the beginners. Secondly, the subjects may have a limited vocabulary and insufficient syntactic structures to call on what they need to communicate in English, and then the subjects would avoid using articles in fearing of misusing them. Finally the subjects lack linguistic competence of English article system i.e. they are unable to determine when and where to use articles.

4.1.2.16 Overextension

This means the redundancy of articles.

11* It makes the flowers open… (…make flowers…)

21* …there are many things in the college. (…in college.)

25* In the senior high school,… (In senior high school,…)

30* …going to the university… (…going to university…)

34* …even the animals will live like in a paradise. (…even animals…)

To explain the errors, we may suppose that the subjects apply the hypercorrection or overgeneralization strategies. Sometimes they are too cautious about articles to avoid using them, and sometimes the students lack linguistic competence e.g. they would apply articles to certain institutions such as school or university.

4.1.2.17 Substitution

This refers to the misuse of 'a' instead of 'the' or vice versa.

46* It became the different face. (It became a different view.)

54* …a first step is… (…the first step…)

Apparently, due to the lack of linguistic competence to distinguish specificity from non-specificity or countability from uncountability, the subjects would commit such errors. In conclusion, though the mother tongue would influence the subjects' acquisition of articles in English, yet generally speaking, it is the subjects' inability to tell one form of article from another form that causes determiner errors.

4.1.2.18 Punctuation errors, Abbreviation errors and Misplacement errors

In the study, the error occurrences in punctuation errors are a little bit higher than expected. A total of 30 errors are found, which constitutes 2.2% of the grand total, and the freshman group commits more errors (18, 3.5%) than the junior group (8, 2.1%) and the senior group (4, 1.2%). As a matter of fact, the Chinese punctuation nearly shares the same forms and functions with the English one. Theoretically speaking, the subjects should have a high command of English punctuation; however, due to the neglect from English teachers and learners, such errors still appear in the study. Examples of punctuation errors are presented as follows.

4*   I hope I can travel all over the world!...and so on. (...world...and so on.)

4*   I always tell me one thing: "If I study...it is impossible"!

(… impossible.")

9* Everyone could go to college! (Everyone could go to college.)

10* I hope, when I graduate… (I hope when…)

36* Of course I don't mean… (Of course, I…)

45* You maybe heart: " A students says: we couldn't…" (You may hear a student say, "…")

53* …music, computer games, TV, programs, and etc. (…computer games, TV programs,…)

63* Why not try to make a wish. (…a wish?)

Interestingly, we can find that the students are inclined to use an exclamation mark (!) to emphasise their points. It could be assumed that once the punctuation system is taught carefully, then such errors could be prevented easily.

In abbreviation errors, a total of 13 occurrences is identified in the study, which constitutes 1.2% of the grand total. However, the errors are all the same one i.e. *J.C.E.E. (Joint College Entrance Examination) in 6, 30, 49, 52, 53, 56, 60, 61, 62, 72, and 73. Interestingly, with the approaching of the Joint College Entrance Examination, the subjects would commit such error more often. In other words, the senior group commits nearly all the errors (10, 3.0%) in the study because they are the ones who will take the examination soon. The reasons why they commit such errors may be due to that firstly the subjects suppose the abbreviation (J.C.E.E.) is universal, which can be understood by all people, or secondly they think that their compositions will be read by Taiwanese readers only, who are supposed to be familiar with this abbreviated term. Such error can be corrected if students are told to spell the whole name the first time when using the term.

Misplacement errors here refer to a word or a phrase which is misplaced by the subjects. In the study, a total of 21 misplacement errors are found, which takes up to 1.7% of the grand total. The junior group enjoys a higher error frequency (8, 2.1%) than the freshman group (8, 1.5%) and the senior group (5, 1.5%). Except the example 8 due to the direct translation from Chinese, it is evident that most errors may mainly result from the subjects' inadequate knowledge about the sentence structures in English, especially the indirect questions. Here are some examples.

8*　It let her more hate boys. (It made her hate boys more.)

18*　I think friend who is a person you can… (friend is a person whom you can…)

21*　The life of college… (The college life…)

41*　However, I like the city in fact. (However, in fact, I like the city.)

42*　…the standard of living… (…the living standard…)

45*　…what you don't know they laugh at… (…you don't know

what they laugh…)

54* Making friend with her usually is… (…with her is usually…)

57* I don't know what is friendship. (…what friendship is.)

4.1.2.19 Violation of the sentence and Verb pattern

A violation of the sentence and verb patters, in this study, means a pattern or a verb is used without following a correct form of its own and thus makes sentences look quite unbalanced, though they can be understood sometimes. A total of 71 errors are found, which constitutes 6.1% of the grand total. The proportion of violation of the sentence (59, 4.7%) is higher than that of violation of verb pattern.

The freshman group seems to have more problems (28 errors, 5.5%) in how to construct a complete sentence than the other two groups (20, 5.3% in the junior group and 11, 3.3% in the senior group). Some of the examples are listed below.

1* I can going to a good college. (I can go to…)

7* I wish I can enter into a good… (I wish I can enter a…)

16* No matter what they are my best friends… (No matter what happens they…)

19* There also has many schools, department stores… (There are many…)

26* I always late for school. (I am always late …)

30* I don't know it's good or not. (…whether/if it's good or not.)

35* …then having so many people going to …. (…people go to…)

54* You can realize her characteristic, what's she like… (…,what she likes…)

56* …to let all people are healthy and… (…people be healthy…)

62* There will have a lot of useful… (There are a lot of…)

In short, the possible reasons to account for the errors may result form the subjects' incomplete learning i.e. the correct usage is not learnt holistically but fragmentally, and partially interference from the mother tongue, especially the sentence pattern 'there is/are…'. Both two patterns 'There is/are…' and "…have/has…' are translated into Chinese as 'you 有'; therefore, students will unconsciously mix up these two patterns into 'There has/have…' inadequately.

4.1.3 Semantic errors: rhetoric and stylistic errors

Broadly speaking, any "ill-formed" or improper expression which may result in the distortion, irritation, ambiguity, illogicality or damage in the meaning of sentences to either native speakers or non-native speakers is classified as a semantic error. In this study, a total of 304 errors is found as semantic errors, including rhetoric errors (160, 13.5%) and stylistic errors (144, 13.5%), which constitutes 24.9% of the grand total (see Table 9).

On the average, the lower grade will commit semantic errors more often than the higher group. This may be due to that when students have insufficient linguistic knowledge in L2, they will mostly depend on what they have already known in their mother tongue. Therefore, many Chinese-laden expressions would appear inevitably, and those Chinese-laden sentences could be found among all three different groups. However, we may also assume that students will commit less and less semantic errors once they continue learning to discover the difference between two languages and then can apply correct and appropriate expressions. That may give an account of why the senior group would commit less semantic errors than the other two groups. Some examples below will presented in four categories.

Table 8: The Frequencies of Semantic Errors

Types of Errors	Freshman (%)	Junior (%)	Senior (%)	Average (%)
Semantic Errors	129, 25.4%	101, 27.1%	74, 22.3%	304, 24.9%
Rhetoric Errors	54, 10.6%	60, 16.1%	46, 13.9%	160, 13.5%
Stylistic Errors	75, 14.8%	41, 11%	28, 8.4%	144, 11.4%
Miscellaneous Errors	7, 1.3%	3, 0.8%	0, 0%	10, 0.7%

4.1.3.1 Run-on sentences

The subjects do not write correct sentences with using appropriate conjunctions due to the lack of linguistic competence about how to organise their complex ideas within a complete English sentence, or partially due to the mother tongue interference.

1* No healthy, it is no thing to have much ideas.

(It is useless to have many dreams without good health.)

11* In fall, it rains like spring, it is not hot, not cold, very comfortable.

(…and the weather is neither too hot nor too cold. It's very…)

23* Since we go to there, we can play and rest, we don't watch TV.

(When we are there, we can take a full rest without TV.)

48* I think that health which can't buy even if more and more money is important as much as nothing in life.

(I think although money is important yet without health money is useless.)

4.1.3.2 Redundancy expressions

The subjects would use two similar words or phrases to express one idea, which may result form their inability to decide which word or phrase is more suitable to use.

5*   …your heart and your body can feel comfortable. (…you can feel your body…)

16* I have many friends, some of them are girls, others are boys. (I have many friends.)

18* …the secret in her heart… (…her secret…)

32* …but they still my best friend and friend. (…are my best friends.)

51* And there is much emotion between people and people.

(There is much more contact among people.)

4.1.3.3 Improper expressions

The subjects would choose an improper word or phrase to express their ideas due to their lack of sufficient linguistic knowledge about vocabulary and phrases in English.

*4   I need to found ideals in my mind to influence myself.

(I need to set up a goal to keep me …)

10* I still think about everything in Taichung, of course my good friends.

(I still miss everything in Taichung, especially my good friends.)

13* …special wishes, I must take them seriously. (…, …make them carefully.)

16* …work hard to change the mistake together. (…to solve the problem together.)

50* …our friendship don't decrease. (…will not change.)

64* Home is organized of people and building.

(A home is constituted with all family members.)

4.1.3.4 Chinese-laden expressions

This is the majority of semantic errors. Many Taiwanese students are used to translating their ideas from Chinese into English directly in the process of writing English compositions; consequently, many English sentences are constructed in Chinese word order, which could be understood only by non-native (Chinese-speaking) readers. This implies that many students would depend on Chinese-laden notions due to their lack of complete linguistic competence in English. Here are some typical instances.

2* My birthday will be happy, too. (I will be happy on my birthday…)

8* There were many problems in her mind, she was never sad outside.

(Although she had too many worries, yet she never expressed them to others.)

12* …she just over senior high school class. (…completed her senior high school education.)

24* In the night, they are together to talk about what happened in the place.

(At night, they will get together to talk about the local news.)

30* In the recent years, the J.C.E.E. would be broken it.

(…would be abolished in few years.)

40* He often give me cold water. (He often discourages me.)

54* …a desire for a period romantic love. (…for temporary romantic love.)

73* I want to release my emotion and go abroad to play with Mom.

(I need to travel abroad with my mother for some relaxation.)

74* I spent little time concerning about the news.

(I spent less time watching TV news.)

4.1.4 Miscellaneous errors

Those errors which could not be classified into the above categories would be termed miscellaneous errors. A total of 10 is miscellaneous errors, which constitutes 0.7% of the grand total. It seems that the freshman group would commit more such errors (7, 1.3%). Below are some examples.

5* …when you go to the ___, your heart and body… (no suggestion)

8* I wan't everybody… (no suggestion)

16* But she stresses the ~~~ between friends.

The above examples cannot be interpreted by me at all based on the context though I have tried my best to judge which exact words the subjects would try to use originally. Other examples are like 19* 公德心 (civism), 22* 個性 (characteristics) and 關係 (relationship). Due to their lack of vocabulary knowledge, the subjects would use some Chinese characters rather than the exact English words. Such errors could be found more frequently in the lower group. The reasons are very obvious i.e. either the subjects have limited vocabulary or they have not learnt these terms yet.

4.2 Findings and Implications of the First Stage Research

4.2.1 Findings

To begin with, generally speaking interference from Taiwanese/Chinese does influence the students' process of writing English compositions, especially in the category of semantic level. In addition, the grammar system in English like the present third person plural 's', prepositions and determiners, which have no Chinese equivalences cause errors, too. There is no clear distinction of determiners in Chinese/Taiwanese. For example, the expression "Give me pen." is acceptable in Chinese/Taiwanese. Besides, the preposition '*zai*' (在) can be used to replace most determiners in English. "The cat is sitting *on* (*zai* 在) the table" and "I am *in* (*zai* 在) the office now." are two instances.

In general, in Taiwan the participants tend to translate their notions directly from Chinese into English when composing writings. In other words, the students would think what they want to write in Chinese first, even note it down in Chinese, and then translate the notes into English word by word. Undoubtedly, many erroneous Chinese-laden expressions could be made without considering the basic difference between two languages. Some teachers' using traditional grammar translation method could be one reason to account for the happening. Thus, it is not surprising that translation method in teaching writing would not be so recommended (George, 1972; Dulay, Burt & Krashen, 1982) for it only strengthens the students' reliance on L1 structures.

Most of the errors counted were due to students' insufficient knowledge of English. Students often over-generalised depending on their previous knowledge of English without realising the limitation of applying these rules. For example, students may write a sentence like "Give me some moneys." after they learn the rule "some + plural nouns". In fact, overgeneralisation and mother tongue interference represent aspects of the same underlying learning strategies. They both "result from the fact that the learner uses what he already knows about language, in order to make sense of new experience" (Lightbown & Spada, 1993: 25). In overgeneralisation, learners depend on their previous knowledge from the target language, while in interference they rely on the previous knowledge on their mother tongue. Students are trying to test their own hypotheses about the language based on their knowledge.

Thirdly, as the error frequencies show, the students in each grade have many semantic problems in their writing. In addition, all the students have more grammatical problems than semantic ones only with a slight difference in each grade. Perhaps we may suppose that those who are in a lower grade would depend on their mother tongue largely when writing and thus make more semantic errors. In a word, the errors students made may then mainly result from their overgeneralisation, simplification of target language, or interlanguage. Although the percentages of grammatical errors in the lower grades (65.5% in the freshman group and 58.6% in the junior group) are slightly less than that of the senior group (70.5%), it does not imply that the lower-grade students have a higher command of grammatical knowledge. It is possible that the students use the avoidance strategy to avoid using what they are unfamiliar with (James, 1998).

Of course, there are probably other reasons causing their errors. They may be 'slip of pen', 'simplification by omission', 'communication strategies' or 'induced errors.' However, these sources cannot be clearly located unless an interview with the participants is carried out.

Fourthly, on average the length of the writings (132 words on average) is close to the requirement set by the Entrance

Examination (from 80 to 120 words). However, the content of these compositions was relatively poor. The students tend to view each topic provided as a narrative topic and were not able to distinguish the different writing styles among the topics. Moreover, there were few innovative ideas found in the compositions. Perhaps writing time is not enough, or there is no task designed for students to generate novel ideas. Other possible reasons may be that

> either they are not endowed with the kind of rich
> ideas that re required for good writing, or they
> may not be able to express in target language the
> better ideas they have in mind (Huang, 1988: 67).

Here is a suggestion for enriching ideas. Students should form a habit of reading more. They should be advised to note down ideas occurring to them in daily life. In addition, teachers should provide students with enough time to discuss topics before writing. This can help students collect and share ideas with other classmates.

Furthermore, teachers could also offer students more opportunities to write. Also, students must learn how to manage their time well in the process of writing.

Many students and teachers in Taiwan do not pay much attention to writing. Some teachers even require students to memorise so-called model compositions, or simply write down a topic on the blackboard and then have students write 'freely'.

In addition, seldom do the students generally check their compositions after writing. What is worse, some students would give up English writing for they consider they can still get high grades in other subjects to enter college without writing a composition. Fortunately, this will be changed soon. According to a new educational policy, English writing is compulsory in order to apply for schools or take further exams.

4.2.2 Implications

As Norrish (1995: 97) suggests, if EA can be applied by teachers with intervals of time, then teachers can have an clear idea about how individual students are progressing and which points they have not learnt yet. For example, the hierarchy of difficulty could be very helpful for teachers to detect students' difficulties in English writing. In this study, we can clearly understand word spelling, verb tense, and number & countability of noun are the most difficult for students in writing as the following hierarchies of difficulties indicate.

Figure 4: The Hierarchy of Lexical Errors

Spelling Errors (70, 5.7%)

1

Capitalization Errors (28, 2.3%)

1

Compound Errors (12, 0.5%)

1

Morphology Errors (6, 0.4%)

Figure 5: The Hierarchy of Verb Errors

Tense Errors (64, 5.5%)

1

Error Usage of Verb (43, 3.6%)

1

Auxiliary Errors (20, 1.5%)

1

S-V Agreement Errors (17, 1.3%)

1

Participles Errors (13, 1.1%)

1

Infinitive Errors (9, 0.8%)

1

Mood Errors (8, 0.8%)

1

Voice Errors (8, 0.6%)

1

Gerund Errors (6, 0.3%)

Figure 6: The Hierarchy of Noun Errors

Number & Countability (73, 9.9%)

1

Pronoun Errors (25, 2.0%)

1

Error Usage of Noun (35, 2.9%)

1

Case Error (11, 0.8%)

1

Gender Error (2, 0.2%)

The errors of word spelling, verb tense, and number & conutability of nouns are all global errors and need direct treatment. Moreover, through EA teachers also can begin to understand the ways in which learners are influenced by the mother tongue and the target language, and the reasons why learners commit errors and how they make errors can be identified (Lee, 1997). Thus different teaching methods to treat such errors then can be adopted as well.

To sum up, as Richards (1974) asserts, EA could be an ideal approach to help teachers understand their students' learning system and their hierarchy of diversity in writing. In the following sections, some implications, deriving from the first stage of the study, for teachers to teach English writing, will be presented together with some implications for students to write effectively.

4.2.2.1 Implications for Teachers

First of all, the essential way to improve the ability of writing is to read a lot and write a lot (Hedge, 1988; Wang, 1996). A teacher should provide students as many opportunities as possible to practice writing, especially in class. However, undoubtedly some students would regard writing as a tedious and painful job and thus fear or reject writing. In view of this, a teacher should try to help learners regain their confidence and change their negative attitudes toward writing. The first step of writing is in no fear of making errors and then keeping on writing and writing again.

Secondly, as Hedge (1988) states, a teacher should create a good classroom atmosphere in class for students to write. That is a teacher can keep good relationship with learners and interact with each other without any barrier. A good way to build up good relationship with students is that try not to look at errors only, once students have satisfying productions they should deserve their teacher's praise and encouragement. As discussed earlier, EA tends to neglect correct productions. Language learners need to be praised, especially when a student demonstrates that he/she is developing accurate production where problems existed before. Although this study focuses on accuracy, it is clear that students can be commended for other aspects of writing, for example, range of vocabulary or overall organisation of the text.

Moreover, a teacher should provide students real chances to experience being writers as well. With such chances, students can discuss to share their ideas and writing with others, have enough time to practice writing, and receive help form their teachers anytime.

Besides, Robb, Steven, and Ian (1986) also state that most EFL teachers' feedback on writings is indiscriminate for they scarcely record students' error types, which then even can make remedial teaching become impossible. As what discussed in the earlier section, knowing students' hierarchy of difficulty can be very useful for teachers to know why students would commit such errors and which problem learners may have in the process of writing. Then the suitable teaching EFL writing method could be adopted to deal with the problems effectively and rightly. In short, for a teacher, keeping a record of students' error types is fairly substantial and advantageous.

Furthermore, from the collected compositions it seems that students would prefer to the narrative topics rather than other ones. This clearly shows that the subjects would avoid those unfamiliar topics due to the lack of confidence and limited argumentative ability. However, the argumentative topics are always the favourites in the Joint University Entrance Exam. This is not to say that teachers should only provide students argumentative topics for the reason of examinations but students should have more chances practicing the argumentative writings. A clear guideline and structure offered to students about how to organise an argumentation might be useful as well, using sources such as White (1986).

Next, in the process of writing, firstly a teacher should provide a purpose, and audience for learners, either real or simulated in a pre-writing stage (Hedge, 1988). Then, enough time for discussing the topic and collecting ideas should be offered. When writing, students should be taught to follow the right direction in their heads. Students should not regard the first draft as the final production. Usually a good writing will be revised and checked over and over to make sure there is no mistake or misunderstanding. Therefore, a teacher should not correct compositions until they have been examined carefully by students.

In addition, the feedback stage may be the most complicated for teachers in the process of teaching writing. Unless a teacher has sufficient time to correct each minor error, a number of techniques for correcting are extremely needed. First of all, a teacher should decide which type of error should be treated immediately. They could be global errors or the linguistic focus of the writing. As to other minor or local errors, they should be left for students themselves to correct. Peer correction might be a good way for students to correct each other's errors for it makes students take responsibility for their own work. Only by treating error correction as a problem-solving activity can students retain feedback (Corder, 1981). Although there are many techniques for teachers to correct errors such as offering students only the hints of the correct forms (Corder, 1967), using different color inks to distinguish the more important from the less important (Burt & Kiparsky, 1972), using self-monitoring (Storch & Tapper, 1996), or recording students' errors in a tape as Farnsworth suggests (in Cohen, 1975), yet the writer personally prefers what Huang (1983) and Wingfield (1974) propose i.e. (1) use coded signs to correct errors rather than provide answers directly, for example, '~' means to change the position of expressions, '^' means something is missing, or 'Art.' refers to article errors, and (2) deal with errors through marginal comments or footnotes. (3) Finally and importantly, a brief comments at the end of each composition is dramatically encouraging e.g. 'Well-done, an interesting story', 'I enjoy your writing', or 'Excellent, I like the words you used.' Besides, the teacher could also commend those aspects of strength e.g. a good range of appropriate vocabulary (see Appendix 7).

Then, after the error correction, the next stage is to provide a number of remedial teaching. If a teacher finds that a type of error is generally committed by most students, undoubtedly an explanation with examples is required in class. Perhaps a number of drills can be used to test if students have learnt it or not. However, if a type of error only belongs to few students, then discussing the error orally with students seems to be enough. Most important of all, the new tactic adopted for remedial teaching should be different form the original writing teaching method (George, 1972).

Finally, teachers should remember that some errors maybe belong to induced errors. Correcting the wrong thing, or the right thing for the wrong reason, or not correcting enough can easily make matter worse (Stenson, 1974). Since in most cases, a teacher is the main corrector of writing errors a teacher himself/herself should be aware that there should be no identified error induced by the teacher such as wrong instructions or incomplete linguistic competence. The best way to avoid such induced errors is that teachers themselves should always enrich their teaching methods and linguistic knowledge; besides, practicing writing more often is a solution as well.

To sum up, writing can be taught successfully and errors can be corrected enjoyably if teachers can always pay attention to their learners' needs or problems in writing and then adopt the best treatment toward those problems.

4.2.2.2 Implications for Students

In the first place, students should not fear to commit errors. Errors could be necessary and valuable in the process of writing. If students can use the error check lists all the time as their teachers record what kinds of problems they have made in the previous writings, then next time when writing, these special categories surely need special notice to avoid committing the same errors.

Next, students need to broaden their horizon. As the study shows, the content of students' writing is quite poor because of their lack of some genuine ideas while writing. To solve this problem, students should develop a habit of reading a lot. Magazines, books, newspapers, Internet, or even their daily life are all good sources of innovative ideas. Whenever a good idea occurs, it should be written down in notebooks immediately. Those notes taken could always be wonderful inspirations in composing a creative writing.

In the process of writing, students should always know the purpose of this piece of work and its audience first. Then, try to make the ideas be expressed as clearly as possible (Hedge, 1988). Of course, an appropriate selection and correct operation of vocabulary and structures are potentially important as well. However, a complex structure is not absolutely better than a simple one unless the former can be used rightly since the more complex a sentence is, undoubtedly and inevitably, the more possibly an error will be made. Besides, always examining the completed compositions to see if there is any mistake or error is equally essential. Remember that drafts without checking should not be viewed as the final productions.

Finally, students should have a more positive attitude toward English writing. They should dismiss the negative attitude that writing English composition is only in order to pass the exams but instead English writing would be more necessary in an internationalised society, especially in looking for jobs. Writing may not be an easy or happy task but it is definitely an exciting work. Why not try to enjoy writing?

4.3 Part B: Discussion and Findings from the Stage 2 and Stage 3

In this section, I will discuss the findings from the questionnaire and the interview. The frequency and percentage of each option in each question is tabulated in Appendix 5.

4.3.1 I like to write something about _____.

(e.g. family, friendship, society, politics,...)

Table 9: The Topics Students Prefer to Write About

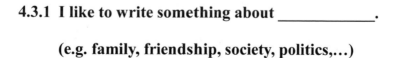

Freshman		Junior		Senior	
Friends	14	Friends	17	Friends	13
Family	14	Family	8	Experiences	13
Experiences	12	Experience	7	Family	9
Life	3	Society	2	Society	2
Emotions	1	Sports	1	Interests	2

Thoughts	1	Life	1	Future Plans	1
		Psychology	1	Sports	1
		Interests	1		

When asked which type of writing topic they preferred, nearly 80 % preferred to write something narrative or descriptive about their friends, families or personal experiences. Only a few preferred an argumentative topic. This result exactly corresponds to the findings in Part A. There are a number of possible reasons. One is that the students do not have sufficient knowledge or vocabulary to compose an argument. Therefore, if they can choose a topic freely, they would rather write about something they are already familiar with in order to avoid errors (James, 1998). The second possibility is that the students have not been taught how to write an argument.

4.3.2 When I read the topic, firstly I will usually_____.

☐*a. think about it by myself (67.2%)* ☐*b. discuss it with classmates (14.2%)* ☐*c. ask the teacher for an explanation (7.5%)* ☐*d. other _____ (please specify) (7.41%)*

From the responses to the question 2, students normally think about the topic by themselves before writing. Students do not often discuss the topic with either teachers or their classmates before writing. Perhaps this may be due to their individual learning style or the time limitation of a writing class.

4.3.3 Do I write an outline?

☐*a. always (11.1%)* ☐*b. usually (24.1%)*

☐*c. sometimes (43.3%)* ☐*d. never (20%)*

About 60% of the students reported that they do not always or usually write an outline before writing. Maybe the problem of 'time limitation' is still a crucial reason. Students are not given extra time to compose an outline. Ms C. said sharply in the interview: *"a beautifully-written outline is useless if the final writing is not completed by the end of the period."*

4.3.4 Will I write in Chinese first and then translate it into English?

☐*a. always (8.3%)* ☐*b. usually (21%)*

☐*c. sometimes (27.5%)* ☐*d. never (36%)*

From the responses to the question 4, we can see that not too many students write English essays depending on their previous Chinese/Taiwanese knowledge. However, the freshmen reported that they more frequently write their essays on Chinese first.

In the interview, Ms C. gave an interesting example of how 'induced errors' may happen during writing (Stenson, 1974). Ms C. stated:

One of my students was misled by her 'Chinese teacher' (a teacher who teaches Chinese) in how to write a topic sentence in English writing. The Chinese teacher suggested the student to leave the topic sentence blank first. Begin writing the rest and then come back to summarise what has been written within one sentence. This sentence is exactly a 'topic sentence' and then it should be placed in the beginning of the paragraph. The Chinese teacher was severely blamed for that mis-teaching by a native-English-speaker teacher.

4.3.5 If I don't know how to choose vocabulary or expression, I will _____.

☐*a. consult a dictionary (60.3%)*　☐*b. ask classmates (6.8%)*
☐*c. ask the teacher (1.5%)*　☐*d. use another expression (29.5%)*

The responses of the question 5 sharply show a different perception between students and teachers. About 60% of the students consult a dictionary, and 30% of them find another expression. They rarely seek help from teachers or classmates. However, in the interview, teachers showed a strong desire for offering students help in their writing. Yet the problem is unless students explain their difficulties, teachers will assume there is no problem at all. In addition, Ms C. mentioned another interesting phenomenon. She said that *sometimes her students came to her for help just because they believed that her answer was more authoritative and correct. Most important of all, she was the marker of their writings. Students were trying to please her and comply with her to get higher grades.* Mr. Y. also said *he even felt guilty if he only helped some students instead of all.*

4.3.6 I believe using correct grammatical usage is ____.

☐ *a. very important (32.3%)* ☐ *b. important (47.8%)*

☐ *c. not very important (17.5%)* ☐ *d. not important (1.5%)*

4.3.7 I believe coherence in writing is _____.

☐ *a. very important (54.3%)* ☐ *b. important (39.8%)*

☐ *c. not very important (4.5%)* ☐ *d. not important (0%)*

4.3.8 I believe handwriting is _____.

☐ *a. very important (25.6%)* ☐ *b. important (43.8%)*

☐ *c. not very important (26.5%)* ☐ *d. not important (2.8%)*

4.3.9 When I finish writing, how many times will I check my grammatical usage?

☐ *a. 0 time (19.3%)* ☐ *b. 1 time (57.1%)*

☐ *c. 2 times (18%)* ☐ *d. more than 3 times (2.5%)*

4.3.10 When I finish writing, how many times will I check my coherence?

☐ *a. 0 time (7.6%)* ☐ *b. 1 time (59.5%)*

☐ *c. 2 times (24.8%)* ☐ *d. more than 3 times (6.3%)*

Questions 6 to 10 examine what students are really concerned about in their writing. Apparently, over 80% of the students in each group regard correct grammatical usage as important or very important. In Taiwan, most students learn English just hoping to pass tests. The grades in an English test represent one's English proficiency assumingly, and correct grammatical usage is very highly-demanded in evaluating. This tradition in Taiwan has been passed down for decades and not changed significantly till now. This also can explain why many students would check for grammatical accuracy directly after writing. This phenomenon is quite contextualised in Taiwan. More strikingly, over 94% of the students consider coherence as very important or important, which is even higher than that of the emphasis on grammar. From the findings in Part A, students also make less semantic errors than grammatical errors.

Another cultural influence on writing can be seen from the responses to question 8. Nearly 70% of the students emphasise the importance of handwriting on their writing. The importance of clear handwriting has been stressed all the time since one begins his/her student career in Taiwan. Most teachers in Taiwan also place high emphasis on it, because teachers believe that handwriting can reflect a learner's character, and can show whether or not s/he is concentrated or puts great effort on learning. Sometimes, a neatly-written composition even with many errors will be sympathised easily. Ms. L. remarked in the interview: *"If a writing is a good piece but with a terrible layout or handwriting, I would be annoyed easily and then unconsciously identified it as many errors, but in fact they are not errors."* Probably this is another sort of 'induced error' in such a context, not from teachers' mis-teaching but from teachers' annoyed emotions.

4.3.11 When I get writing returned, firstly I will look at

_____.

☐*a. the grades (60%)*   ☐*b. the errors (9%)*
☐*c. the comments (23.1%)*

From the responses to the above question, we realise that students are mainly concerned about their grades after they received writing returned. Cultural factors possibly play an influential role in such hierarchy. In Taiwan, it is 'grades' that determine which university a student can enter and how his/her academic status is ranked in class. Furthermore, parents may not clearly know if their children have a good command of English writing or not. Therefore, they judge children's English proficiency by the grades. Ironically, students are in fear of facing errors but it is errors that judge their ability in English.

4.3.12 When seeing the corrections on my writing, I will usually _____

☐*a. ignore the corrections (28.3%)*   ☐*b. correct the errors right away (46.3%)*   ☐*c. wonder why (6.5%)*

Surprisingly, there are so few students who would like to know why they made errors on their writing. Most of them simply follow the corrections on the essays, and then correct the errors immediately. The freshmen reveal a higher percentage of correcting the errors right away (59.5%). However, this does not necessarily imply that the students will not make the same errors in the future. Usually, students just simply correct the errors according to the correct usage written by their teachers on the essays. Both Ms C. and Ms L. mentioned in the interview: *"I had tested it before.   There is no use of offering correct usage. The exactly same errors do re-appear in the next essay."*

4.3.13 Please rank the possible reasons causing my errors from 1 to 5. (1: the most possible; 5: the least possible)

☐*Chinese/Taiwanese interference (3)*

☐*incomplete knowledge in English (1)*   ☐*poor writing skills (2)*

☐*slip of pen (4)*   ☐*affective factors (5)*

Question 13 shows how students attribute the sources of their writing errors.   Generally speaking, this hierarchy is quite the same as the results of previous research. The implications of such ranking will be discussed in details in the section of 4.3 Implications.

4.3.14 I would like my teacher to correct each error.

☐*a. strongly agree (34.3%)*   ☐*b. agree to some extent (57.1%)*

☐*c. disagree to some extent (7.5%)*   ☐*d. disagree (0%)*

4.3.15 I would like my teacher to provide each correct usage?

☐*a. strongly agree (45.3%)*   ☐*b. agree to some extent (38.6%)*

☐*c. disagree to some extent (2.8%)*   ☐*d. disagree (0%)*

4.3.16 I would like my teacher to let me correct errors on my own?

☐*a. strongly agree (7.5%)*   ☐*b. agree to some extent (28.5%)*

☐*c. disagree to some extent (53%)*   ☐*d. disagree (12.5%)*

4.3.17 I would like my teacher to take all responsibility of correcting my errors?

☐*a. strongly agree (17.6%)*   ☐*b. agree to some extent (41.1%)*

☐*c. disagree to some extent (32.1%)*   ☐*d. disagree (7.8%)*

From the responses to the above questions, we can see that over 90% of the students (Q. 14) on average agree that teachers are supposed to correct each writing error and provide corrective usage for students. In Taiwan, a teacher is usually viewed as the only provider for correct knowledge; students are the passive receivers simply. Moreover, many teachers in Taiwan believe that correcting each error is a kind of criterion of being a good teacher. Not only teachers have such a demand of themselves, but parents and students also have the same expectation of their teachers.

There may be another reason accounting for this. Students assume that their linguistic knowledge is not sufficient to correct errors and even if they can, they cannot ensure correctness. Moreover, though Lightbown and Spada (1993) assert that 'global/major errors' are supposed to be corrected by teachers and 'local/minor errors' should be left for students to correct, students and teachers in Taiwan tend to view each kind of error equally serious. Both of them commonly believe that "an error is always an error no matter if it is a global/major or local/minor error, because each error will result in equivalent deduction of marks in tests."

Even when asked what comments they would like on their essays, many students reported that they are eagerly to know where they went wrong and how to avoid making the same errors next time. They rarely ask for the comments on their ideas on the essays. This cultural factor is greatly related to the status of using English in Taiwan. Many students in Taiwan believe: "English writing is just a compulsory subject to take in order to pass an exam."

4.3.18 I would like to do peer-correction?

☐*a. strongly agree (6.3%)*   ☐*b. agree to some extent (32%)*
☐*c. disagree to some extent (37.3%)*   ☐*d. disagree (22.6%)*

The statistics shows that not too many of the students are willing to try 'peer-correction'. There are a number of possible reasons. One is that students do not believe that their classmates are capable of dealing with their errors. Secondly, due to a demand of privacy or shyness, students are not so willing to share their writings with others in public. In fact, students do not hope their peers to know their shortcomings in writing. Senior high school is a stage full of competitions in Taiwan. Students are so competitive with each other in order to enter a good university. These reactions are indeed very culturally influenced.

4.3.19 Errors are unforgivable and must be corrected right away.

☐*a. strongly agree (11%)* ☐*b. agree to some extent (46%)*
☐*c. disagree to some extent (31.6%)* ☐*d. strongly disagree (9.8%)*

4.3.20 Making errors just reflects I am learning, and improving.

☐*a. strongly agree (56%)* ☐*b. agree to some extent (42%)*
☐*c. disagree to some extent (1.1%)* ☐*d. strongly disagree (0%)*

It is quite interesting if we compare the results of the above two questions. On the one hand, students still strongly responded that errors should be corrected immediately; on the other hand, they also reported that making errors should be viewed more positively. The responses to question 19 are still culturally-influenced, but those to question 20 show that students now are more willing to take a positive attitude toward errors. Perhaps, students believe that errors have been taking control of learners and teachers for such a long time and now it is time to face them more bravely.

4.4 Implications of the Second Stage and the Third Stage Research

In this following section, I would like to offer English teachers in Taiwan with a number of points drawn from the findings of this study about how to make writing activity more meaningful and effective.

Firstly, it seems that there is a huge gap between students' favourite writing and writing in the Entrance Examination. In fact, teachers could provide students with more opportunities in writing a logical argument. This is not because the Entrance Examination favours argumentative writing but it can help students learn how to develop their thinking logically and express their personal views about the world around them. Writing is more meaningful if it can reflect what students think about their world.

Secondly, it may be fruitful for teachers if they can allow students some time to discuss the topic before writing. By discussing with others, students can learn to appreciate others' ideas, and become more willing to share their own ideas with others. In this way, the writing atmosphere becomes more humanistic rather than mechanic (Hedge, 1988).

Thirdly, there should be more reliable and trustworthy interaction between teachers and students during the process of writing. Students should be encouraged to talk with teachers while writing. However, they must also be encouraged to be autonomous. This means that students should learn to solve their problems first, and if in vain then they can always turn to their teachers for advice.

Moreover, just because correct grammar is highly demanded in Taiwan, it is quite easy for students to neglect the importance of meaning in writing. This would result in many erroneous or Chinese-laden expressions e.g. *He often gives me cold water (correct: He is often discouraging me.). Usually, the longer students learn English, the more careful they will be with meaning of their writing. In fact, 'coherence' is equally important in writing. Quite usually, a semantic error will seriously change or block the original meaning and thus causes misunderstanding. If writing is a communication tool for students to express their thoughts, then obviously meaning is more important than grammar. This is not saying that teachers should on the contrary allow no error at the semantic level, but that since language is viewed as a communication tool, the clear transmission of meaning is more requested.

Next, over 60% of the students reported they would check and revise their writings before submitting. However, the proportion is still not high enough. Sometimes, the time limitation is a crucial reason. As Edge (1989) suggests, teacher should encourage students to revise and recheck their writings before submitting. This means that students should not regard the first draft as final writing. Re-checking writing helps students to detect a number of errors by themselves, especially those performance errors such as careless spelling or wrong punctuation.

Furthermore, it could be argued that the purpose of English writing could be defined as knowing students' ideas about something. Hence, ideally there should be no grades at all on writing except teachers' comments. Each learner's idea should be respected and valued equally, and thus 'marks' is not suitable to be used to evaluate or assess the ideas dogmatically. In Taiwan, students would easily take it for granted that low grades mean that the teacher does not like the essay or even does not like students themselves. Students usually relate the grades to teachers' preferences. However, if teachers have no choice but to give a number of marks to indicate students' abilities in writing due to some pressure, here are two suggestions. The first one is that the teacher marks two different grades on each essay: one is for the degree of manipulating correct grammar, and the other is for the degree of how clear the essay conveys its semantic meaning. Alternatively, the teacher could clearly explain in advance to their students that 'the marks' is not related to the value of ideas on writing, but only to the degree of how they use English correctly.

In addition, if teachers hope error correction to be useful and effective, implanting some continuous teaching could be helpful. Norrish provides a number of suggestions. He (Norrish: 1995) proposes that teachers should provide remedial teaching after correction by using another teaching technique. "Remedial teaching carried out as a result of the findings of an error analysis should use a different approach from that tried for the initial teaching activity" (Norrish, 1995: 97). Unfortunately, this advice might be neglected easily because of teachers' excuse of time pressure in teaching.

According to the findings from question 13, the lack of English proficiency is the main source causing errors in writing. It seems that many high school students do not have confidence in English writing. Obviously, they are in need of a number of long-lasting motivation and appropriate mediation in English writing. Many Taiwanese senior high school students believe: 'English writing is only a compulsory subject to take in order to pass tests.' In this situation, a teacher's role in facilitating learners' motivation in English writing would be definitely crucial.

In Taiwan, finishing a short English essay in order to pass exams appears to be an extrinsic motivation for learners. However, if such motivation can be transformed into an intrinsic one, then writing can become a process of enjoyment rather than a vocation of unhappiness. To do so, teachers are advised to "present tasks which tap into learners' intrinsic motivation both at the stage of initiating and sustaining motivation" (Williams & Burden 1997: 125). However, personal interest, curiosity, challenge and the development of independent mastery and judgment should be taken into consideration carefully as well.

Besides, to establish a comfortable atmosphere for writing in which there is no fear of making errors is equally stressed. Teachers can encourage learners to read more and write more without fearing making errors. Then, teachers themselves might also change the perception of being teachers. They could build up interactive relation with learners in a writing class. The easier way is trying not to focus on errors only but trying to praise any learner's progress either in good linguistic performance or invaluable ideas (Hedge, 1988).

Over 61% of the participants attribute their errors to interference from Chinese/Taiwanese. Nevertheless, such kind of interference should decrease when a student learns more. It is generally believed that the longer students learn English, the more likely they realise the specific rules of it and the less possible they will depend on their mother tongue.

Interestingly, compared with other two groups, the freshmen showed a higher tendency in attributing their errors to affective factors. If success in writing depending on sufficient linguistic knowledge is defined as internal attribution, then it seems that the lower grade students would easily attribute their failure to external factors- - something they are unable to control. Ms L. in the interview provides her explanation to this phenomenon: *'The freshmen have not been used to a new learning environment yet and they are still searching their way out to English writing. They certainly become more nervous when exposing to such an uncertain condition.'*

'Performance error' is the least likely reason causing writing errors, identified by the students. These errors could be lessened if students can be advised to check their writing before they submit essays.

In Taiwan, though competitions among high school students are so intense, 'collaborative learning' cannot be considered impossible at senior high schools. On the contrary, it could be developed as early as possible i.e. starting from the elementary school stage. As long as a sense of trust could be set up between each learner, then to effect collaborative learning in senior high school will become more plausible. At present, the education authority in Taiwan also has come to realise the importance and necessity of 'peer learning' at each learning stage. Hence, a number of policies are being taken accordingly to reduce the intense competitions among each student. The decision of abolishing the entrance exam is one of these. The situation is changing gradually towards a positive side.

Finally, the responses to question 20 clearly show an encouraging changing attitude towards errors from students. Though over half of the students agree that 'errors are unforgivable and must be corrected right away', what is more inspiring is that over 95% of the participants identify making errors as a signal which represents they are learning and progressing. Since the learners take such constructive perception towards errors, it is time for teachers to retrospect the attitudes towards errors, too. There is no denying that errors may usually result in a sense of discouragement or incapability. However, what teachers can do is trying to transform these unhappy feelings into a positive encouragement. Once a learning environment with no-fear-of-errors is set up in classroom, meaningful interactive learning atmosphere between learners and teachers might work automatically.

CONCLUSION

CHAPTER 5

CONCLUSION

In conclusion, though EA cannot be quite helpful in telling students how to avoid making errors in learning a language, yet

> EA can be especially useful if repeated on comparable tasks with intervals of time in between. It gives teachers an idea about how individual students are progressing through their Interlanguage and indicates any points which have generally not be learned (Norrish, 1995: 97).

The purpose of this study is not to locate the sources of writing errors and then prescribe some therapy to 'cure' all the errors. On the contrary, it asserts that teachers should acknowledge that making errors is quite inevitable for students in learning a language. Making errors clearly reveals that students are learning and are testing their hypotheses to make sense of their language world. This should be considered as an encouraging phenomenon for teachers. "Our job as teachers is not just point out differences between our students' language and standard language. This is too negative a role" (Edge, 1989: 13). Teachers should provide learners with more opportunities to show what learners can do with the language they are learning and encourage the growth of the language by appreciating the learning steps (Norrish, 1995; Edge, 1989).

Playing a traditional role, a teacher in Taiwan is not supposed to tolerate students' errors. However, this old-fashioned role may need a number of imminent changes. Teachers, students and parents all need to have humanistic tolerance to learners' errors. Though the status of using English in Taiwan will not be changed within a short period of time, cultural influences on language learning can be refined gradually with the development of emphasising individual values and ideas.

REFERENCES

Brooks, N. (1964). *Language and Language Learning.* New York: Harcourt, Brace and World.

Brown, H. D. (1987). *Language Theory and Classroom Practice.* Toronto: The Ontario Institute for Studies in Education.

Burt, M. K. & Kiparsky, C. (1972). *The Gooficon: A Repair Manual for English.* Rowley, MA.: Newbury House.

Chen, C. C. (1979). *An Error Analysis of English Compositions Written by Chinese College Students in Taiwan.* Unpublished Ph.D. dissertation. Austin: University of Texas.

Chiang, H. H. (1999). *The Analysis of Grammatical Errors Made by Speakers of Chinese in Written English.* Unpublished MA dissertation. Coventry: Warwick University.

Chiang, P. J. (1993). *How to Improve English Compositions Teaching in Taiwan's High School: A Study of Error Types and Strategies.* Unpublished MA dissertation. Kaohsiung: NKNU.

Cohen, A. D. (1975). Error Correction and the Teaching of Language Teacher. *Modern Language Journal, 59*: 415-422.

Corder, S. P. (1967). The Significance of Learners' Errors. *IRAL, 5*: 161-170.

Corder, S. P. (1981*). Error Analysis and Interlanguage.* Oxford:

Oxford University Press.

Deng, K. S. (1987). A Study of errors in English tense committed by senior high third year students. In *Papers of the Fourth Conference on English Teaching and Learning in Taiwan (pp.353-373)*. Taipei: Crane Publishing.

Dulay, H. C. & Burt, M. K. (1974). You Can't Learn Without Goofing: An Analysis of Children's Second Language 'Errors'. In J. C. Richards (Ed.). *Error Analysis: Perspective on Second Language Acquisition.* Harlow: London.

Dulay, H. C., Burt, M. & Krashen, S. (1982). *Language Two.* New York: Oxford University Press.

Edge, J. (1989). *Mistakes and Correction.* Harlow: Longman.

Ellis, R. (1994). *The Study of Second Language Acquisition.* Oxford: Oxford University Press.

Ellis, R. (1995a). *Understanding Second Language Acquisition.* Hong Kong: Oxford University Press.

Ellis, R. (1995b). *Instructed Second Language Acquisition.* Oxford: Blackwell.

Fathman, A. K. & Whalley, E. (1990). Teacher response to students writing: focus on form versus content. In *Second Language Writing: Research Insights for the Classroom (pp.178-190)*. Cambridge: Cambridge University Press.

Fries, C. C. (1945). *Teaching and Learning English as a Foreign Language.* Ann Arbor: University of Michigan Press.

George, H. V. (1972). *Common Errors in Language Learning*

Insights from English. Rowley, MA.: Newbury House.

Hedge, T. (1988). *Writing.* Oxford: Oxford University Press.

Henderickson, J. M. (1978). Error Correction in Foreign Language Teaching: Recent Theory, Research, and Practice. *Modern Language Journal, 62* (8): 387-398.

Huang, T. L. (1974). *A Contrastive Analysis of the Syntactic Errors in English Made by Chinese Students and its Implications for the Teaching of English Syntax to Chinese.* Unpublished Ph.D. dissertation. Carbondale: Southern Illinois University.

Huang, T. L. (1983). *Applied Linguistics and Teaching English Language.* Taipei: Crane Publishing.

Huang, T. L. (1988). *Performance Errors and Teaching EFL Composition: A General Teaching Model.* Taipei: Crane Publishing.

Jain, M. P. (1974). Error Analysis, Source, Cause, and Significance. In J. C. Richards (Ed.). *Error Analysis: Perspective on Second Language Acquisition.* Harlow: London.

James, C. (1998). *Errors in Language Learning and Use: Exploring Error Analysis.* New York: Addison Wesley Longman.

Johnson, K. (1996). *Language Teaching and Skill Learning.* Oxford: Blackwell.

Lado, R. 1976. *Linguistic Across Cultures.* Michigan: Ann Arbor,

University of Michigan.

Lee. C. Y. (1997). *An Analysis of Errors in English Compositions Written by Selected Military Cadets: Its Implications for Teaching EFL Writing.* Unpublished MA dissertation. Taipei: Fu-hsing-kang College.

Lightbown, P. & Spada, N. (1990). Foucs-on-form and Corrective Feedback in Communicative Language Learning: Effects on SSL. *Studies in Second Language Acquisition, 12*: 429-448.

Lightbown, P. & Spada, N. (1993). *How Languages are Learned.* Oxford: Oxford University Press.

Nemser, W. (1974). Approximative Systems of Foreign Language Learners. In J. C. Richards (Ed.). *Error Analysis: Perspective on Second Language Acquisition.* Harlow: London.

Norrish, J. (1995). *Language Learners and Their Errors.* Hong Kong: Macmillan.

Politzer, R & Ramirez, A. (1973). An error analysis of Spoken English of Mexican-American pupils in a bilingual school and a monolingual school. *Language Learning, 23*: 1.

Richards, J. C. (1974). *Error Analysis: Perspectives on Second Language Acquisition.* Harlow: London.

Richards, J. C., John, P. & Heidi, P. (1998). *Longman Dictionary of Language Teaching and Applied Linguistics.* Hong Kong: Longman.

Robb, T., Steven, R. & Ian, S. (1986). Salience of Feedback on Error and Its Effect on EFL Writing Quality. *TESOL Quarterly, 20* (1): 83-93.

Robinson, L. (1969). *Teaching Writing.* Paper given at the Third Annual TESOL Convention, Chicago, Illinois, March 5-8.

Schachter, J. (1974). An Error in Error Analysis. *Language Learning, 24* (2): 205-214.

Schachter, J. & Celce-Murcia, M. (1971). Some Reservations Concerning Error Analysis. *TESOL Quarterly, 11*: 441-451.

Selinker, L. (1972). Interlanguage. *IRAL, 10* (3): 209-231.

Stenson, N. (1974). *Induced Errors: New Frontiers in Second Language Learning.* Rowley, MA.: New bury House.

Storch, N, & Torch, J. (1996). Patterns of NNS Students Annotations When Identifying Areas of Concern in Their Writing. *System, 24* (3): 323-336.

Tso, F. F. (1993). *Explorations in Applied Linguistics: Papers in Language Teaching and Sociolinguistics.* Taipei: Crane Publishing.

Wang, L. K. (1996). How to Teach Chinese Students Writing. *The Proceedings of the Fifth International Symposium on English Teaching.* Taipei: Crane Publishing.

Wardhaugh, R. (1970). The Contrastive Analysis Hypothesis. *TESOL Quarterly, 4* (2): 123-130.

White, R. V. (1986). *Teaching Written English.* London: Heinimann Educational Books.

Williams, M. & Burden, R. L. (1997). *Psychology for Language Teachers: A Social Constructivist Approach.* Cambridge: Cambridge University Press.

Wingfield, R. J. 1974. Five Ways of Dealing with Errors in Written Composition. *ELT Journal. 29:* 311-313.

Ying, S. Y. (1987). *Types of Errors in English Compositions by Chinese Students: A Search for Interlanguage.* Unpublished MA dissertation. Taipei: Fu-jen Catholic University.

Yang, W. H. (2004). The Problems of An A. *2004 The Proceedings of English Language Teaching & Translation (pp. 115-125).* NPTSU: Ping-tong.

APPENDIX

Appendix 1: Topics Provided for Writing

Please pick any one of the following topics to write a short English composition; if you don't like any of them, you can decide your own topic. The length is around 120 words. You need to finish your writing within 40 minutes.

1. My Birthday Wish/ My Millennium Wish

2. My Hometown

3. Two Friends

4. Are Too Many People Going to College?

5. How to Keep Your Boy/Girl Friend?

6. School Sounds

7. Other (Please decide your own topic)

Appendix 2: Sampled Compositions

1. My Birthday Wish

My birthday wish is I can going to a good college after one year. I like art. So I can going to college about art. And I hope I can be an art teacher. So I had to study very hard. Aspecially English, there are many books about art are English. I must study English well is order to read them. But it is much important now I must studying hard to finish my wish. I believe I can be success.

The other wich is my family bodies are very well. Healthy is money. No healthy, it is no thing to have much ideals. It is important to have good healthy.

2. My Birthday Wish

Everyone has different birthday wish, and I'm on exception. I have many wishes in my every birthday, but most of them can't be come true. At first, I hope I can buy a Bass. Because I like to play it. It can make me happy and relife. But it's so expensive that I can't buy it. Second, I want to buy some clothes. It is more easy to come true. And my parents can buy me one or two clothes. Third, I hope that my family and I can get together to eat a cake. This feeling is so wonderful that I can't foreget easy. Although this wish that I hope to come true, I more wish my family and friends can wish me "Happy Birthday", that's enough. May birthday will be happy, too.

3. My Home Town

My Home Town is in Kaohsiung, Which is a convenient city. I live there, and I could get more information than other city. Of course, it doesn't include Taipei. Because it is more convenient than Kaohsiung. If I live there, I could get more fashional information and go some funny places. But I still like Kaohsiung than Taipei. Why? Because Kaohsiung is my home town. I was born in here, and I also understand how wonderful it is. Kaohsiung is quiter than Taipei. And live there is more comfortable. Because there doesn't have much noise, much cars. And doesn't have much people crowded, so I like Kaohsiung than Taipei.

4. My Birthday Wish

In my birthday, I enjoy giving me a hope by meself. For example, I hope I can study more harder now than previously, don't fish in the troubled water; I hope I will enter a good school after two years; I hope I can travel all over the word…. And so on. In my birthday, I always tell me one thing: If I study hard, I will enter a good school. If I don't do it, it is impossible"! So in most important, I need to found ideals in my mind to influence myself. Because it can let me do better.

5. My Home Town

My hometown is in Tainan. There are many old buildings, culture and good foods in Tainan. People in Tainan are friendly. You can ask them anything about Tainan and history of there. You also can visit many interesting places and then eat some good foods. When you go to the your heart and body can feel comfortable because there are many farms, kinds of farmers, trees and etc. Although the city is getting older, Taiwan's culture and history are presurved in here. Therefore. It is an important city in Taiwan.

6. My Birthday Wish

My birthday wish is almost the same each year. I only wish that my family can be happy and healthy. But I have a special wish when my eighteen birthday. Because my eighteen birthday is after JETT so I want to travel. To travel all over Taiwan. I think that travel maybe can give me different knowledge. And I also want to have a boyfriend. Because I want to feel another feeling and that can help me to write. Maybe all the wish are not so special but I really hope them come be come true. So now I have to study hard and then my parents will let my go to travel all over Taiwan. And my last wish is that my family can be happy and health every day.

7. My Birthday Wish

I wish I can enter into a good college. I think it is every senior high school students' hope. If I work hard it must be came true. And I wish I can be happy everyday everywhere, and so do my family and friends. Happy is the most important thing in life. And I wish my parents can take much money. It is good for everyone in my family, especially me. Because I very enjoy playing and shopping, these cost much money. At last, I wish these three hope can come true. These are all my Birthday wish.

8. Two Friends

When I am in junior high school, I have two friends Anny and July. They were my best friend. We always talked to each other. In school, we always talk about our problems to each other and we will sove it together. Anny was a beautiful girl. Many boys liked her. But she didn't like boy. She thought boys were dirty and bad. She was very angry. It let her more hate boys. She was very confuse this. July was different. She never confused this. I always heard her laugh. Her grades also very good. She seems never have problems. But when we talked about ourself. I found she didn't a happy girl. There were many problems in her mind. She was never sad outside. I don't know we lived happily or unhappily. My best friend, Anny and July, are always confuse and the other laugh. I wan't everybody how I know what they thought.

9. My Birthday Wish

My birthday was in 11. 20. It's a wonderful day. I'll have many friends to celebreat for me. Gifts, cakes,… and my birthday's wish. Now, if today was my birthday, I wish I could go to College with Zoe, Cimone… and all of my friends. It's our dreams, our further, our all. It's why we went to study senior high school. If the wish could be true, and my friends and me wouldn't study, everyone could go to College! It's impossible. And I know if I want to College, I have to study, study, study!

10. My Hometown

There is a beautiful place in Taiwan, the weather there is very well and people are very friendly, there is my hometown, Taiching! I was born there, and lived for eleven years. In downtown, there are many many department stores, and coffee shops everywhere. I came to Kaohsiung seven years ago, because of my father's business. When I left Taichung, I was very sad, and I hope someday I will be back! I still think about everything in Taichung, of course my good friends. I hope, when I graduated from College, I want to look for job there. The place was full of my beautiful memory. I like there just like love myself.

11. My Hometown

There are many trees, flowers, birds, and so on in the country. The country is my hometown. People lives there are very friendly, because their life is happy and comfortable. The street doesn't have so much cars in cities. The air are frish, because there are many trees, and flowers which are very beautiful. The weather there are change very soon… In spring, it rains not very much, bnut it makes the flowers open. In summer, it rains very very much, but it is still too hot to stay there. In fall, it rains like spring, it is not hot not cold very comfortable. In the last season, it rains a little. It makes we must to wear move clothes. This is my beautiful hometown. I love my hometown.

12. Two Friends

I have two best friends. I know them when I in elementary school. They are Emma and Anne. Anne and I live on the same street, if I want to go to her home, I just spent three minutes. Emma went to New Zealand three years ago. She is my best friend. We know each other for nine years. Everytime I have trouble, I always tell her, and she will help me with her best. We have write letters to each other, but she is in Taiwan now, because she just over her senior high school class.

13. My Birthday Wish

Do you have any wishes? I have lots of wishes, like no wars, being healthy, getting more money, being beautiful, playing basketball better, being taller, and …having more wishes! But the birthday wishes are special wishes so I must take them seriously. The first of my birthday wishes is everyone has healthy body. The second of them is I can do anything better. And the last one is I can smile every day.

14. My Birthday Wish

My birthday will be coming up. It's on November eighth. On that day, I hope someone can buy a cake and sing birthday's songs for me. Then I dream my birthday wish. I have two of my birthday wishes. One is entering in good collages, and another is having a girl friend soon. I really hope that the two wishes will come true! Of course, I know to enter in good collages must study hard, It's not enough to have a wish. But another wish I hope the god can give me a nice girlfriend!

15. My Hometown

My hometown was far away the big city because this factor makes it quiet. There were many green trees and beautiful houses in this little country. My hometown was my memories of the childhold. There was a tall tree in front of my house where there were few cars and people pressing. I often played games with my brothers under this tree, and I sometimes climb this tree to look at other places far away. There was a river near my hometown was long and clear, and its water was too clear to drink so where there were many fish to caught up. This was one of the places where I often played at my childhold. My hometown had many trees, beautiful houses, clear rivers, and relatives. This is my most beautiful memories in my life, and these things full of my childhold not to make me forget it forever.

16. Two Friends

I have many friends. Some of them are girls, others are boys. But two of the friends are my good ones. One is Penny, and the other is Shalion. Both they are my classmates, also my the best friends. But they are diffent in some places. Penny is a good students and treat everyone very well. So I like her because of her friendly. Shalion is also a good students, but doesn't treat everyone well. She can treat someone unfriendly because she doesn't like that person. But she stresses the ~~~ between friends. She can give anything up to help friends when they are in trouble. So I like her courge which can help people anytime. Both of them are a little fat, but Shalion likes sport, Penny doesn't. I can get some things from them. The things may be good, may be bad. But we can work hard to change the mistakes together. No matter what they are my best friends in my life.

17. My Birthday Wish

I wish I can go to Japan. Because there are many places, like Tokyo, etc. There we can go shopping and see many different people from different countries. That is interesting to me. And I also wish I can go to college. Because if I don't go to college, I will not easy to find job after I finish my senior high school. So I must be hard in senior high school. And I also wish my family's bodies health and everything fine. But I don't think I only have three wishes. I want many wishes, like, but all kind of bags, eat different ice cream, have a lot of money, etc. But everyone say we don't have a lot of wishes. Because God say, everyone have only three wishes. But there is one thing confusing to me. That is why I wish don't carry up. When I ask my father or mother. They will say we should work hard and they will come true. But I wish I can carry them up this time.

18. Two Friends

I think friend who is a person you can believe deeply, and help you lot, but sometimes it can't always be true! And if it happened that will hurt you much. And if you are really good friends, no matter how far he or she is, you can still close. My best friend always talk to me about the secret in her heart and so do I. But we are a kind of distant friends, so we can't talk too often. But we are knowing each other's personality so much. I think that's why we are close and getting together. Friends is a thing you should have. If you don't, you'll feel sad in your life!

19. My Hometown

It is a beautiful place but has many noises. There has many cars, motorcycles, trach, and people in every street. There also has many schools, depement stores, and factiries. I like it, though it is noise, busy, and so on. But I don't like the traffic. It is too crowded. And people are not 公德心. The heavy traffic makes people not comfortable. The government should make laws to fight it. In recent years, teenagers have more and more entertainments. The city is busier and busier.

20. My Birthday Wish

If I can wish on my birthday, I wish my dream will come true. I always do many dreams, some are possible, some are difficult. For example, sometimes I want to be a beautiful fashion designer, I can design many kinds of clothes and I also become a beauty with my clothes. But I understand it doesn't come true, because I don't have so big power to catch everybody's heart. Sometimes I hope to be a bird, because I can fly all over the would, I can see many thing, When I'm tired, I take a rest in a tree and eat sweet food. But it can't come true. Now, I have a big wish, I have to do myself. Maybe the answer is "Yes", maybe it's "No". I don't tell anyone until my dream come true. I make effort to study step by step.

21. Are Too Many People Going to College

There are a lot of people who want to go to college. Why? Because there are many things in the college. People can get much more knowledge and join many clups. The life of college is very interesting. We can go to class only one day, two days, three days or four days. But it is not good. And before entering college, we must pass a exam. The exam is to test us if we can go to college. There are many people who have passed the exam. They can go to college, but there are still some people who don't pass the exam. Of course, they can't go to college. And there is one thing that going to college is helpful for us when we will want to work in the future.

22. Two Friends

I think friends must to love to believe. And they must to

know about each other's mind, thinking and 個性. The other one must hope that she can trust each other. And always believe her, that can be good friend. I'm very hated that if someone don't believe me. That will break my heart. I feel that if good friend don't trust you, then nobody that you can trust. And I think "Two friends" is a very closed 關係. They can talk about their hope, their future, their dream and their mind. Most important is she can keep my secret and give me some suggest. So I think friendship is found on "believe".

23. My Hometown

My hometown is in Loucra, it is a country. There are many rivers and mountains, when I was free, I can go mountain climbing or swimming. I always do that with my brother. It is very quiet, and the people is friendly in there. If my family go to there, we always live with my uncle. In there, we can do anything. But the TV programs is very pool. Sinces we go to there, we can play and rest, we don't watch TV. Because there are too many things waiting for us. If we are free, we always go to there. Not only there is very quiet but also we like there.

24. My Hometown

My hometown is in Kaohsiung. It's a quite place, but, sometimes there are many baby crying in the morning. In the place, people are nice and friendly, but, they always talk a lot. In the morning, people go to the park together; they go to dance, walk, and talk. In the night, they are together to talk what happened in the place. There are two park in my hometown, and there are many children playing there, it's a beautiful park. There are two elementary schools, which I had studied. There are a lot of funny thing in the place. I like the place, because it's many thing what happened in my life and many friend in the place. But, there are some bad thing, I hate like crying, speaking loudly. I can't sleep well, because these.

25. Are Too Many People Going to College

In the senior high school, most of student want to go to college. Why? For their job. If they had even study in college, they can find job easy. Generally speaking, college was hard to join. If you want to go, you had to study hard. But now, our government make it easy to go to college. The first one, they built many college. Second, they make the person who want to go to college become better in senior high school. Third, they also built many others school for student to change. Because this, about 65 percents senior high school students can go to college. But is it good? I don't think so. Many students in college only play in all their college life. When they go out to work, they also don't know how to do were better. In my mind, to be a good worker is more important to be a student, isn't it?

26. My Birthday Wish

My Birthday wish is to have a motorcycle. Because I must go to school by bus now. But the bus driver's attitude is very bad. They often shout to you loudly and don't stop at each bus stop. Sometimes I go to bus stop early, but I always late for school. Why? Because the bus doesn't come, they often come after twenty minutes, even thirty minutes. Because of the bus, I always late for school. However, if a have a motorcycle, I wouldn't late for school. Besides this wish, I also hope that I can become maturer. If the dream will come true, I can handle any problems easily.

27. My Birthday Wish

I believe that people have a lot of wishes with the age, no surprised, I am, too. First, I hope that the world is peaceful, everybody will wish like that actually. But people know that college exam plays an important role in senior high student's heart, and which college you study may effect your future in Taiwan. Then, money is much useful on earth, so people love it. I love money, too. It can be used in many ways. On real, I want to have a tour of Europe, also, but I don't have lots of money and time, my English is not good at all. I thought if you work harder, then wishes are not be wishes, it can be came true one day, and also I'm working hard to try to make them real.

28. My Homeland

That was obscure, my homeland, where I spent my childhood, seems unreachable. It was the world of love and peace and the land I always long for. Standing alone in the forest nearby a lake, the water there was transparent. Looking through the reflections of the trees and blue skies, live never told any lies. Flying across the land, I fluttered my little wings. Wandering along the lake, I heard the whisper of the wind. Lying down on the roof, I looked up into the dark. It was not dark, shiny, sparkling, and splendidly bright were the eyes of the sky. When I heard the sound of the wind, I could see the tears within. I sailed across the water, float across the sky, my homeland suddenly became a dream where I could never ever find.

29. My Two Friends

I have many friends in school. One of them is Zoe. She's very kind to everyone. She's thin, and her face is very long so we call her "cow". She does everything carefully. Before, her dog, Be Be, diedi she was so sad because she loved it so much. She cried and cried, and I felt sad, too. The other one pf my friends is Cimone. She's a little bad because she likes kidding very much. She has many facial apperances and she's very funny.

30. Are Too Many People Going to College

    Before several years, high school students' goals are going to the university. But now, we think going to school is normal. There are more and more universities. In many people's point of view, if you wanted to get a good job, you should take master's degree, or doctor of philosophy. This thing represented the civiticen's education are getting higher and higher, but the bad thing is that everyone has university. In this situation, if we weren't entering to university, it is too redicilous. In recent years, the J.C.E.E. would be broken it. I don't know it's good or not. The exam is not limited in many several text books. It's a good thing for clever students, but not suited for the student who studied very harder. If I were him, we wouldn't read the book at the desk, and watch TV and newspapers and magazines more often. I think it's not bad.

31. My Two Friends

    I known many friends at school from elementary school to high school. Some of my friends who are very bad go to play computer games and some of my friends who are very diligence study books every day, but the friend I like most is quient and don't like to talk. They are two my good friends in my class. There must be someone asing why I like them. The main fact is that they are very quient lets me feel very cool and inquired. The second fact is that my opinios are many and always consider my opinios correct so my friends I like most are quient and have no opinios.

32. Two Friends

I have one best friend and a friend, Lisa and Linda. They are very different, although they both don't talk too much.   Let me tell you how different they are. Lisa is a very smart, quiet, careful person. She always wants her things to keep cleaning, always do anything well and she also very well-organised, a little bit moody, but she is really a nice guy, speaking to her you'll feel happy. Linda is a very funny, stingy, and a little bit crazy. She always speaks funny things, act some funny actions, she is also enthusiastic in doing anything. Wow! How different they are! Although they have different characters, but they still my best friend and friend!!!

33. My Hometown

My hometown is a beautiful country. There are many tall trees and colorful flowers and kinds of bird's sound and fresh air and green grass. The people are very kind and friendly. Because they will talk to others friendly when we visited there. And we will buy many cheaper things. For example, apples and candies and so on, so we can go shopping. This is my hometown – a beautiful country and I never forget it.

34. My Birthday Wish

I have two birthday wishes. One I hope the world will be peace forever, and there will be no wars, violence and blood. All the people will live like in a paradise, and even the animals can get along with each other peacefully. The other one is that I will get happiness and healthy because the society is too terrible and also more and more pollutions are increasing. I have less power to prevent or improve it. I can't do anything about it, so I just "wish". Anyway, my two wishes might not come true, but I will make them on my birthday every year.

35. Are Too Many People Going to College

It seems that now every student in senior high school in Taiwan has a chance to enter a college, no matter it's a pubilic one or a private one. You enter a senior high school, you study for three years, and you graduate and take the entrance exam. You then have a rate of 60% or more of possibility to enter a college. But is it really good that almost everyone get a chance to enter a college?   I think the answer is negative. To have everyone joining college seems a great development on our education. But since that not every college is fine enough, how can you guarantee that a student from college sure is a wonderful one? We have many colleges now in Taiwan and I believe that there will be more in future. If we can't provide better quality of colleges, then having so many people going to college might not be a good idea. I, as a senior high school student, do not agree that too many people entering college. Besides, the reason above, one main reason that I disagree is because I "am" a senior high school student. Isn't there a saying goes, "Human is always selfish."?

36. How to Keep Your Boy Friend

Two people love each other, but what the point is how to be together in good relationship. I think whether girl or boy, you shouldn't think your girl or boy friend is "Yours". Of course I don't mean you have to share your girl or boy friend with others but he or she also needs some room. How to keep your boy friend? You shouldn't lie to him and love him with your true heart. There's one thing important: Your boy friend is not your dog or your doll! You can't treat him like your pet or toy, this mean you shouldn't limit what he wants to do. He can have his own friends, he can do the thing he likes to do. You may say if he loves the other girl just because you give him too much room! If this thing really happens, the factor is that your boy friend and you don't trust each other and in fact, you guys got the communicated problem. Getting along with your boy friend is just like how you get along with your friends. There are many similar things between these two things. I feel that it's not a big deal to be with your boy friend. Don't think too much or always doubt something. How to keep your relationship needs communication, trust each other, so you don't worry you will lose him!

37. My Birthday Wish

Wonderful! My birthday is around the corner - - September 23. On my birthday this year, I will make a wish that I can enter my dream school and major in English which is my interest. Ever since I attended junior high school, I have been fascinated by English! It is impossible to deny that English is useful to everyone; whatever one does, he/she can't do without English. The reason I make such a wish is that I want to keep updated all the time, and English can help me achieve my goal because it can broaden my horizons and enable me to keep up with the times. Little do I want to make a wish that I will get large amounts of pocket money from my parents, or that I will meet my dream girl. On the contrary, I just wish to enrich myself and then to become well-educated. This way, I have to better myself so as not to be disillusioned with this golden dream - - to acquire knowledge!

38. My Hometown

My hometown, Tainan, is located in south Taiwan. The weather here is warm. However, while typhoon strikes here, it becomes cold, rainy and rains dogs and cats. Tainan has many farms in which produces rice for exportation and many sub-typical fruit. It is famous for its old buildings including Confucious Temple, Cheng Cheng-kung's Temple and so on. Therefore, Tainan is a traditional city in structures. I like Tainan very much because most people lives here are always very friendly and they always give others sweet smiles. I feel the human touch that they shows deeply. I am very lucky that my hometown is Tainan where I gain the most warm.

39. My Hometown

My hometown, ping-dong, is located in south Taiwan. It is mostly surrounded by some mountains and farms. So it always like green-paradise. Because my hometown is in a tropical zone, the weather there is very hot and humid. Because of that weather, my hometown also has very much kinds of fruits, like mango, pineapple, bananas and so on.

Such beautiful flowers and sweet fruits make my hometown more special and popular with visitors. Because the young people don't like working on farms, my hometown has a very big problem. You can see the old men and children everywhere, because the most of young people have gone out working in the big cities. But I still believe that the bad situation will be better in the future. I love my hometown, not only because it's beautiful scenery, but also because it is the most friendly and helpful place.

40. Two Friends

Jack and John are two of my friends. Jack treat me very well. He always laughs with me and give me a hand. I'm so lucky that I can make a friend with him. John and I usually get along well. But he treat other friends better then me, I suppose. Not only did I talk to him but also play with him. He often give me cold water. We three are known each other. Whether how he consider me, I still want not to lose John. He is a interesting person when I know him at first. Friends are help to each other. We three ever got into trouble and solved together. That is, a friend in need is a friend indeed. So they are not only my friends but also like my brothers.

41. My Hometown

My hometown is Kaohsiung which is located in

southwest Taiwan. It is the second big city in Taiwan. In the evening, it looks like a big house which is full of light. So I very like the sight in Kaohsiung in the evening. And the weather in Kaohsiung is very good. It is not as cold as that in Taipei in winter and is not very heat in summer. However, it is a problem which I am thinking that the problem is serious. The problem is heavy traffic. I spent much time coming back home everyday. So I hate the heavy traffic better. However, I like this city in fact. I like it because it is better than Taipei in many poets.

42. My Hometown

My hometown, Kaohsiung, is a famous industral city in Taiwan. It has the biggest seaport - - Kaohsiung Port, and it has many beautiful scenery. Because it is a modern city, so I never feel lonely. There are so many places to enjoy myself. For example, department stores, galleries, theaters, stadiums, etc. Just it's an industral city, so there are many environment threat, such as air pollution, noise pollution. These problems affect not only our life quality but also the standard of living. Generally speaking, it is also a busy city and brings many convenience for our daily life. Hense, I live my country.

43. My Hometown

My hometown, Kenting, is located in south Taiwan. It is

mostly surrounded by mountains and sea. The weather in my hometown is very hot. The big sea, white bench and pretty mountains make my hometown more beautiful. In recent years, there are more and more visiters come here. So Kenting is more and more lively. Because there are more and more people come here to play, the environment is getting polluted. The news reported the coral reef is also polluted. So we should do our best to stick up for our environment. If you love it, don't do damage to it.

44. My Hometown

My hometown, Small Ryukyu, is located in southwest Taiwan. It is a outlying. Most people live by fishing so we can eat fresh fish. It is always very hot because it is in a tropical zone. Many people come here to travel every weekend. Population became less and less because they moved to other countries to work. I love my hometown where have blue sky, widely sea and fresh air.

45. School Sounds

In School, we can hear many different sounds. Like dogs's sounds. Birds's sounds, students's sounds and other sounds. When you go alone in classroom, you maybe heart: " A teacher says: we couldn't go to travel for our school", this is a compland sound. Look another place, there are some students that they are laughing. What you don't know they laugh. Over a little time, two dogs bark and run each other; to near they is very danger, so it is better to go away now. To across some classroom, and a Teacher is anger, he, roal in his classroom, you can think these students test not good. School sounds' include love, angry, cry and happy. When you go around all this school, you maybe find many different interesting thing.

46. My Hometown

My hometown is a country. There are many farmer on farm. There is little noise, so it is very quiet. In my childhood, I used to playing on my farm or at school. At that time I often fish and carry fish in the rever near my home. I like the kind of living very much. But with my grewing, it became the different face. There are nothing in the rever but population. Recently it happened to many trash's wars. It goes without saying, I don't like so. I hope that it will return the country I used to be.

47. My Birthday Wish

I have three birthday wishes. First, I wish my family are always healthy and happy. We can help one another, talk about our daily life, solve problems and even make funs. Second, this is very important to me - - passing the Joint

College Entrance Examination smoothly. And choose the subject that I am interested in. Then find my favorite job. Third, this is a great ideal - - world peace. After all, the most important thing is that you have take actions and not to give up. Coming true your wishes or dreams is not far as long as you want to do them all out and a little extra. I have three birthday wishes, and I hope they will be come true.

48. My Birthday Wish

My birthday wish have two at 20 age. First one is that I wish my family and friends is very good for health. I think that health which can't buy even if more and more money is important as much as nothing in life. Another one is that I wish the longer my father lives, the happier he is. Because not only he brings me up but also he does everything for me and let me feel love of family. So I am full of thank to my father.

49. Are Too Many People Going to College

There are too many people going to College. Concerning the education, it has become more and more popular than before. Because of it's popularity, there are many students taking part in the J.C.E.E. every year. According to the population of students is increasing, the school is increasing, too. It may cause a lot of problems, like competition. Everyone wants to have job, but everyone has the same standard (all graduated from college). Therefore, they many compare their grades or schools. And it may lead to a high 失業率. In conclusion, there are really too many people going to College.

50. Two Friends

I like to make a friend with many persons. Two persons of my friends are closely that met in junior high school. They are kindness, active, smart and always give a hand to someone who needs help. One of them likes English and always gets good grade in it. But the other is not, she is supposed that English often makes her have a bad headache. She likes sport much, especially basketball. Much as them have not interests in common, yet both of they are my dear friends. Maybe we don't often communication with each other, our friendship don't discrease. When summer or winter vocation, we will get together and talk to each other.

51. My Hometown

I was born in "Shinwu". Here is country, there are a lot of farm. There is fresh air in "Shinwu". Although there is no Seven-Eleven, but I like it. "Shinwu" is not a convenient place, but it had a lot of thing that city didn't had. It is fill with green. And there is much emotion between people and people. We like our neighbors, and we care each other. My Hometown did not like advanced city. It did not have all kinds of convenient thing, but the people who live here almost like it. Because "Shinwu" is my Hometown, our Hometown.

52. My Birthday Wish

On year of two thousand's birthday, I have several dreams and some purposes. I wish I can make my dream come true. First, I can pass the J.C.E.E. in the summer. And then I have a wonderful life in the college. The other is my family and my friends are safe and happy. I am the third years of senior high school students. As time goes by, I should face to the J.C.E.E. soon. It is an important time of life. I deeply wish I can join a good university and have a more freedom in the college life. And the other wish is my family and my friends are safe and happy. After several mouths, I may study in the college which far from home and live outside. I can't take care with my families. I hope they can life happy and without unfounture. I wish I can atten to my purpose. I most study harder and harder. That are my birthday wish.

53. School Sounds

It's a little rounded world where I study. There is less

and less frictions unless they and I are still strengh. At class we speak those lessons because teachers ask us to do. during free time in school, we talk to each other about sports, music, computer cames, TV, problems, and etc. When most students are talking to another, maybe it becomes noise or otherwise. Through talking, one kind of communication, I find it exciting to make friendship with some people whose interests are as the same as mine. The most importance is to express our thought. So the sound from our talking is by no means any kinds of noise. contantly, it seems to be one clever singing around everyone's ears. But now we'll be ready to J.C.E.E., there is little sounds here for studying. The month of July in which it could change every student will come soon, and this school sounds from our talking might also be took away. I have no idea to speak this feeling that I take right away. Therefore, the friction is no outcomes.

54. How to Keep Your Girl Friend

Many young people always have a desire for a period romantic love, but those who know the true love are less and less. Making friend with her usually is a first step, and you can realise her characteristic, what's she like, and try to make her happy by talking with her often or writing to each other. You'd better learn to forgive her, and find out the outcomes on the quarrelsome. It's usually the main secret which keeping a love long to communicate frequently. If you love more with your enthusiasm, the more you'll get it from the love. The true love is base on friendly treatment!

55. Two Friends

I have two friends, one is called Monica and the other is Angela, we were all studied in YANG-MING senior high school. At first, let me make the sketch of Monica. She is very cute, and having the large voice, and so does her laughing. As far as listening her laugh, you will be happy. In addition, she is a good student who is study very hard and pays attention in class. Another good friends of mine is Angela. She is like a lady. She is more quiet than us. And she is such a beautiful girl, there are many boys in our school all like her. She has the long hair, big eyes and good grades. Monica likes mountain climbing, running, swimming…etc. Angela likes to go to movies, look at books, writing…etc. And I often sing, play basketball, shopping. Although we have different interests, we are the best friends. We often go shopping, see movies, study with each other. We were young, pretty, and happy girls. In this time, We have the same desire which is we all can be the students of universy after three months. And now, the word, "To win out, we must first believe that we can." Is said every day.

56. My Birthday Wish

Last year's birthday, I was a senior high school student, so I wished I could pass the J.C.E.E. next summer. At the very moment, I'm studying hard all the more for entering the college. Many friends around me encourage me to study in the library where is quieter. My teacher also keeps telling me that don't give up at the last moment. The suggests that everyone offers to me are very helpful. If I make my dream come true, I would thinks my friends, teachers and my parents because they realise the college is important for me. Now, I have had an idea that I will make my this year's birthday wish to let all people are always healthy and enjoy their every day.

57. Two Friends

When I was a junior high school student, I don't know what is friendship. Because I was a shy boy and I studied in a school that was regarded as the strictest school. So all I have to do in school was studying and studying. Not until did I go to senior high school, I finally found the friendship. Now I know two friends, one is Mary another is Jay. They treat me considerate. I am glad to know them, and I will treat them considerate too.

58. My Hometown

My hometown is located by the sea. Although it is small and poor, it's peaceful. I like my hometown. That is where I grow up. In my childhood, I used to play with my neighbors. I had a lot of fun there. I always went fishing at that time and brought my family many fish. I often pick up shells and play them by the sea. It's not like general cities. There are very few young people staying there, because they learned there to city to find better occupations. Thus, the people who are living in my hometown almost are elderly people or children. Although it is so, I still like to live there. It is my hometown.

59. My Hometown

My hometown is located in Nankan, Taoyuan. The first time you go there, you will find the traffic much more heavy. Because the only shopping mall in Taiwan is there. Besides it, the international airport is not too far from Nankan. When visiting Nankan, you can find people there are kind and like to do others a favor. And also you can see many foreigners, because the Evergreen Company is located there. Nankan has good traffic systems. It is very convenient to go anywhere from Nankan. So that Nankan is more and more prosperous. And I believe it will be very soon.

60. Are Too Many People Going to College

There are more and more universities in Taiwan in proportion to the promotion of education. Of course, it is a wonderful fact for students in senior high schools. But the level of those who can pass the JCEE is getting lower as to the increase of many private colleges. I suppose it is very vital to education in Taiwan. In fact, college-graduated students are the ones who will arrange our country on many respects, such as diplomacy, finance and so on. They are involved on those social freshmen seriously. Thus, students are choosen in JCEE if they are the real persons have potentials. The outstanding ones have the right to go to college. Therefore, it is the best way to develop potency with proper-number universities. Otherwise, our country will fail gradually as a result of two many college-graduated students.

61. My Birthday Wish

About ten days ago, I just celebrated my eighteen birthday. On that day, I as usual make three wishes and I dream that I will carry them out. The first wish is that I want to pass the JCEE, choice my favorite college to study, and then major in the subject I am interested in. After doing that, in the long summer vacation, I want to learn how to drive, how to use computer and something I have to learn. Because in such use, and I don't like to waste it, so I should find some meaningful thing to do. This is my second wish. And the final wish, I thought it is a secret of mine, so let me put in into my heart until make it come true.

62. Are Too Many People Going to College

Are too many people going to college? No, I don't think so. In this kind of age, the society should provide more and more chances to people who want to study more. Therefore, it won't too many people go to college until everyone has got enough knowledge. It's fair to every student who takes part in the J.C.E.E. because if you want to go to college, the only way is to study hard. On the other hand, the man who has got into the college are succeed by his hardly- studying. If more and more people go to college, there will have a lot of useful man and make our country better and better. If the amount of people who can go to college is so little, why do we study so many years? Therefore, I don't think too many people go to college.

63. My Birthday Wish

I have ever made many wishes, to be a basketball player, to travel whole world, to be wealthy, to be a billiard professor and many other wishes. Why I have so many dreams? I think people have different thoughts in each age. Maybe, some of these dreams will not be come true. But, there's still some hopes in my mind, even came to the end I don't work out any of them. Perhaps I can't make it, but they are the target to keep me going more meaningful, and decorate my all life. So, if you felt your life was so boring, why not try to make a wish.

64. Other

What's the difference or connection between a "house" and a "home"? Usually house and home both mean "the place where we live and belong to". That is, we stay in a certain place everytime need to rest, and we call that place a "house" or a "home". However, we can't call a "house" as a "home". A house is only a construction which has no feeling, but when we call someplace as a "home", that place must filled with love and warmth. Home is organised of people and buildings. While love exists, a cottage can be a home. With no love, a mansion is nothing but a house. It is love that make home differ from house.

65. Other

Jane had been a happy girl until her classmates made a school prank on her. Once, she was a healthy girl; however, now she can't walk on her own. Watching this news on TV, I felt shocked. I saw a girl with no smile but permanent pain. She faced the reporters without cheer or any other emotions.

My heart soon broken Why? Wasn't it just a prank? Why did it take a girl's happiness? I don't think that student doing such a think would like the affair going on such way. She wasn't on purpose! Of course, no one will be on purpose. However, it's a wrong behavior! If a student would like to be more familiar with other students, it's really not the only way. He can talk with them, play with them, exchange ideas with each other and so on, but he just can't play school pranks casually. Because everyone always don't know what will happen to him! If he thinks it's only nothing, just a trick, he may be sorry for what he did. But the harm is caused, no one can stop it or turn it back as nothing happens.

66. Other

A tall and beautiful girl at the tender age of 14 should have had a lot look forward to in life. But Jane (not her real name) has to spend the rest of her life paralyzed from waist down. It all because of a school prank. A classmate expectedly pulled her chair out when she was about to take her seat. Then three or fourth months later, she couldn't stand up anymore. Some people always enjoy playing a prank to others without thinking what might happened then. It's very dangerous. People may be like the girl paralyzed. I think that the best prank only makes of the victim and the prankster happy, and no one will get hurt. The hidden consequences are so dangerous that you can never image it.

67. Other

Pranks can appear to be fun, but it can be a dangerous trap. When we run around in the classroom; we shout, run, jump, we may easily get hurt because of our excitement. Playing is fun, but if someone isn't careful, he may get hurt or hurt others. I think choice the right places to play is very important. Like the classroom, it's not a good places for playing, because it's too crowd and there are many chairs and desks, if we are not careful we'll get hurt easily. And another is our attitudes, when we are playing, we should be careful and shouldn't be too excited. Because you don't what it would to be when you are too excited. We should remember such examples, and worn ourself. I think no one would bear such accident to whether you are the victim or the prankster.

68. Other

Near-sightedness is a serious problem among the youth of our country. According to a newspaper report, eighty percent of junior high school students wear glasses. In fact, in one school, few students' vision is normal. We use eyes to watch TV, study lessons, see beautiful scenery, but don't take good care of them. We really should notice this problem. I have some suggestions for solving this problem. First, teachers should decrease students' homework, tests, and exams to let them use eyes less. Second, set the auto-turn-off system in every television. If people sit too close to TV screen, it will turn off itself. Third, parents should limit the time that children watch TV and also have to take them out to watch some green plants. If we can do all these things, the rate of near-sightedness will decrease in a few years.

69. Other

I start to believe my teachers. Every teacher all said that we should get good grades in school. I believe it, and work hard. Maybe I am deligent I always get good grades. And then I got good grades in an entering junior high school exam. I was arranged to the gifted class. I had used to be put pressure. Since I go to the senior high school, I was suddenly free, no one will force me to study. But at this time, I lost my way, I don't know why I study so hard that I lose my health. I didn't know what was I persued. I didn't study hard, I lost my confidence. OK! I think I shouldn't complain about it anymore. I should look forward the future.

70. My Millenium Wish

My millenium wish is that my painting skill can improve.

When I wrote something, I always felt that there were

something which I couldn't express. However, I don't know what it is. Every time I try to express this feeling but I didn't do very well. And it's bad than writing. Even though I have rich thoughts. I can't express without skill. I will learn more skills, and paint harder. More over, I wish I can find what is true beauty.

71. Other

When I was a little baby, my family lived in a rented house. My father worked hard in order to buy a house and make our life better. He often worked from to midnight. Sometimes I couldn't see him all day because when I got up, he already went to work and when I went to bed, he yet came home. Now we live in a warm house because his effort. My father doesn't drink and smoke. He will give the money he earns to my mother. He is a model husband. He doesn't hit children. Everytime I make a mistake, he doesn't publish me. On the contrary, he will tell me what I should to do to compensate and not to do that again. Although he is neither rich nor handsome, in my mind he is the best father on earth. I am proud of him.

72. My Millennium Wish

My millennium wish is that I can enter a college which I want. I think, to be a college student should be interesting.

Because I can join many kinds of different clubs and a lot of activities. Besides, I can work part-time to earn my allowance on my own. But I get a big problem. It is that I have to pass the JCEE. I am afraid of the exam because they are very hard to me. I think that's maybe because I did not work hard. I did not concentrate on my work. But I believe if I can work harder and harder everyday, my dream will come true. And in the year 2000, I will be a college freshman.

73. My Millennium Wish

In this new year, there are many wishes waiting for me to finish. But most of them that I want to finish is pass the JCEE and go to the college. And then I can solve and do what I want to do – to be free. Because in the passed year, I always studied, studied, and still studied every day. It made me feel the life very dull. So, as long as the mean time passes, I want to release my emotion and go abroad to play with Mom. Although I have many unknown challenges and troubles to face, I still believe that "As long as I am waking, I have a lot of chances to work out them.

74. Other

My little brother is an excellent student. Although he is just a junior high school student, there is no denying that he is smarter than me. For him, preparing exams or tests is easy, so that he has more time to obtain knowledge from magazines and novels. I spend little time concerning about the news, while he knows almost every universal news and local news. In addition, he likes to play computer games, and I am not very interested in using computers. In my view, he is not only cute but gifted. Therefore, I am proud of my little brother.

75. My Millennium Wish

Millennium year may be special for someone but not for me. In my view, this year is the same with the other passed years. I have a common and simple wish. I wish I could live happily and do my every jobs well. First, I must look the light side of everything. Thus, I can own my happy life and the people around me can also feel happy. Secondly, I will try best of my jobs. My jobs are not very much but study. From now on, I must study very hard so that I can enter a good college. This is my responsibility and job. Consequently, I must practice them by myself. They should not be a wish. I must make them come true as soon as I can.

Appendix 3: The Questionnaire Used by the Students

Dear Students:

Many thanks for your time to do this questionnaire. My name is Yang, Wen-hsien. The purpose of this questionnaire is to understand your attitudes toward errors made in your written English. Your comments would be very useful for my study.
Thanks for your help!

****

Part A:

Please tick or write your information below

1. I am a ☐boy, ☐girl.

2. I am studying in _____high School.

3. I am a ☐freshman ☐junior student ☐senior student.

■■

Part B:

Please tick a box or write down your information

1. I like to write something about _____.

   (e.g. family, friends, society, politics,…)

2. When I read the topic, firstly I will usually_____.

   ☐a. think it by myself   ☐b. discuss with classmates

☐c. ask the teacher for explanation

☐d. other _____ (please specify)

3. Do I write an outline?

   ☐a. always   ☐b. usually   ☐c. sometimes   ☐d. never

4. Will I write in Chinese first and then translate it into English?

   ☐a. always   ☐b. usually   ☐c. sometimes   ☐d. never

5. If I don't know how to choose vocabulary or expression, I will

   _____.

   ☐a. consult a dictionary   ☐b. ask classmates

   ☐c. ask the teacher   ☐d. use another expression

6. I believe using correct grammatical usage is _____.

   ☐a. very important   ☐b. important   ☐c. not very important

   ☐d. not important

7. I believe coherence in writing is _____.

   ☐a. very important   ☐b. important   ☐c. not very important

   ☐d. not important

8. I believe handwriting is _____.

   ☐a. very important   ☐b. important   ☐c. not very important

   ☐d. not important

9. When I finish writing, how many times will I check my grammatical usage?

   ☐a. 0 time   ☐b. 1 time   ☐c. 2 times   ☐d. more than 3 times

10. When finishing, how many times will I check my coherence?

   ☐a. 0 time   ☐b. 1 time   ☐c. 2 times   ☐d. more than 3 times

11. I will submit _____ to my teacher.

☐a. the first draft ☐b. the checked and revised one

☐c. the re-copied but not revised one

☐d. other _____ (please specify)

∎∎

Part C:

Please tick a box

1. When I get writing returned, firstly I will look at _____.

☐a. the grades ☐b. the errors ☐c. the comments

☐d other_____ (please specify)

2. When seeing the corrections on my writing, I will usually

_____

☐a. ignore them ☐b. correct them right away

☐c. wonder why ☐d. other _____ (please specify)

3. To what percentage, do I believe my writing errors may come from the interference of Chinese/Taiwanese?

☐a. more than 90% ☐b. 60%~80% ☐c. 20%~40%

☐d. less than 10%

4. To what percentage, do I believe my writing errors may come from incomplete knowledge in English?

☐a. more than 90% ☐b. 60%~80% ☐c. 20%~40%

☐d. less than 10%

5. To what percentage, do I believe my writing errors may come from poor writing skills?

☐a. more than 90%　☐b. 60%~80%　☐c. 20%~40%

☐d. less than 10%

6. To what percentage, do I believe my writing errors may come from "slip of pen"?

☐a. more than 90%　☐b. 60%~80%　☐c. 20%~40%

☐d. less than 10%

7. To what percentage, do I believe my writing errors may come from affective factors (e.g. anxiety, nervous, excitement…etc.)

☐a. more than 90%　☐b. 60%~80%　☐c. 20%~40%

☐d. less than 10%

8. Please rank the possible reasons causing my errors from 1 to 5.

(1: the most likely; 5: the least likely)

☐Chinese/Taiwanese interference

☐incomplete knowledge in English　☐poor writing skills

☐slip of pen　☐affective factors

Part D:

Please tick a box

1. I would like my teacher to correct each written error?

☐a. strongly agree　☐b. agree to some extent

☐c. disagree to some extent　☐d. disagree

2. I would expect my teacher to provide each correct usage?

☐a. strongly agree ☐b. agree to some extent

☐c. disagree to some extent ☐d. disagree

3. I would like my teacher to correct major errors only?

☐a. strongly agree ☐b. agree to some extent

☐c. disagree to some extent ☐d. disagree

4. I would like my teacher to let me correct errors on my own?

☐a. strongly agree ☐b. agree to some extent

☐c. disagree to some extent ☐d. disagree

5. I would like my teacher to take all responsibility of correcting
my errors?

☐a. strongly agree ☐b. agree to some extent

☐c. disagree to some extent ☐d. disagree

6. I would like to do peer-correction?

☐a. strongly agree ☐b. agree to some extent

☐c. disagree to some extent ☐d. disagree

7. I need more comments than corrections?

☐a. strongly agree ☐b. agree to some extent

☐c. disagree to some extent ☐d. disagree

8. I hope the comments on my writing will be

_____

Part E:

1. Errors are unforgivable and must be corrected right away.

☐a. strongly agree ☐b. agree to some extent

☐c. disagree to some extent ☐d. disagree

2. Making errors just reflects I am learning, and improving.

☐a. strongly agree ☐b. agree to some extent

☐c. disagree to some extent ☐d. disagree

3. To me, writing errors are_____

(please use nouns)

4. Writing errors will make me feel _____

(please use adjectives)

Appendix 4: English Composition Topics of Joint University Entrance Examination from 1986 to 2005

Narration:

1986: Shopping Experiences

1989: On My Way to School

1993: Near-Sightedness

1994: Making Decisions

1999: A Happy Ending

2001: Something Interesting about a Classmate of Mine

2002: The Most Precious Thing in My Room

Process:

1992: Time

2004: (Pictures Writing)

2005: (Pictures Writing)

Comparison and Contrast:

1995: A House Is not a Home

Cause and Effects

1987: Heavy Schoolwork

1988: The Importance of Trees

1990: How to Protect Wild Animals

1991: The Importance of Clock/Watch

1996: Why do You Want to Enter College?

1997: You Win Some; You Lose Some, That is Life

1998: Saying "Thank You" and "I'm Sorry" Frequently will
       Make You a Happier Person

2000: My Biggest Problem in Learning English

2003: Music Is an Important Part of Our Life

Appendix 5: The Results of the Questionnaire

	F: a	J: a	S: a	A: a	F: b	J: b	S: b	A: b	F: c	J: c	S: c	A: c	F: d	J: d	S: d	A: d
B.2	61	67.5	71.5	67.2	23.5	9.5	8.5	14.2	8.5	12	13.5	11.5	7	9.5	5	7.4
B.3	17	15	1.5	11.1	21	27	24.5	24.1	47	26	57	43.3	13.5	30.5	16	20
B.4	4.5	6.5	14	8.3	34	18.5	10.5	21	37.5	18	27	27.5	22.5	38	47.5	36
B.5	65	70.5	45.5	60.3	4.5	7.5	8.5	6.8	4.5	0	0	1.5	23.5	20.5	44.5	29.5
B.6	21	33.5	42.5	32.3	43	63	37.5	47.8	31.5	2	17.5	17.5	3	0	1.5	1.5
B.7	31.5	63	68.5	54.3	59	33.5	29	39.8	10	2	1.5	4.5	0	0	0	0
B.8	24.5	31.5	21	25.6	31.5	39	61	43.8	39.5	23	17	26.5	3	5.5	0	2.8
B.9	17	19.5	21.5	19.3	64	63	44.5	57.1	17.5	14	22.5	18	0	2	5.5	2.5
B.10	6.5	15	1.5	7.6	67.5	61	50	59.5	17.5	18.5	38.5	24.8	6.5	4	8.5	6.3
B.11	17	25	17.5	19.8	67	60	68	65	15.5	14	13.5	14.3				
C.1	55.5	53	71.5	60	13.5	8.5	5	9	29.5	17.5	22.5	23.1				
C.2	36.5	42.5	60	28.3	59.5	47	32.5	46.3	3.5	9.5	6.5	6.5				

C.3	3	0	5.5	*2.8*	52	69.5	55	*58.8*	42	27	28.5	*32.5*	1.5	2	5	*2.8*
C.4	37.5	48	63.5	*49.6*	50.5	38	34	*40.8*	10	13	1.5	*8.1*	0	0	0	*0*
C.5	25.5	19.5	34.5	*26.5*	31	54.5	31.5	*39*	35	25	31.5	*30.5*	7	0	1.5	*2.8*
C.6	1.5	9.5	1.5	*4.1*	34	21.5	37	*30.8*	37	50	22	*36.3*	25.5	17.5	38.5	*27.1*
C.7	32.5	12	12.5	*19*	25.5	31.5	24	*27*	25.5	26	50	*33.8*	14	29.5	12	*18.5*
D.1	33	33.5	36.5	*34.3*	48.5	65.5	57.5	*57.1*	17	0	5.5	*7.5*	0	0	0	*0*
D.2	37	41.5	57.5	*45.3*	58.5	53.5	40	*38.6*	3	4	1.5	*2.8*	0	0	0	*0*
D.3	1.5	9.5	14	*8.3*	24	12	8	*14.6*	59.5	75	66.5	*67*	13.5	2	1.5	*5.6*
D.4	4.5	15	3	*7.5*	41	22.5	22	*28.5*	49.5	55.5	54	*53*	3.5	5.5	19.5	*12.5*
D.5	12	15	26.5	*17.6*	54	37	32.5	*41.1*	33	41.5	22	*32.1*	0	5.5	18	*7.8*
D.6	4.5	13	1.5	*6.3*	31	36	29	*32*	54	29	29	*37.3*	8.5	20.5	39	*22.6*
D.7	36.5	39	59.5	*45*	54	48	36.5	*46.1*	6.5	12	1.5	*6.6*	1.5	0	1.5	*1*
E.1	10	5.5	17.5	*11*	50	50	38	*46*	27	33.5	34.5	*31.6*	11.5	9.5	8.5	*9.8*
E.2	50	65.5	50	*56*	47.5	31.5	50	*42*	1.5	2	0	*1.1*	0	0	0	*0*

F: Freshman   J: Junior   S: Senior   A: Average Percentage

a. b. c. d.: The Choice a, b, c, d

B.2: The Second Question in Part B

C.1: The First Question in Part C

C8: Please rank the possible reasons causing my errors from 1 to 6 (1: the highest; 6: the lowest)

		Freshman	**Junior**	**Senior**
Highest	Interference from MT	7	3	4
	Incomplete English Knowledge	25	22	25
	Poor Writing Skills	5	6	9
	Slip of Pen	0	1	0
	Affective Factors	4	0	1
Lowest	Interference from MT	3	3	3
	Incomplete English Knowledge	1	0	0
	Poor Writing Skills	0	0	1
	Slip of Pen	11	7	10
	Affective Factors	26	20	22

E3: To me written error is a/n _____. (Please use a noun.)

Freshman		Junior		Senior	
Learning	28	Learning	27	Learning	30
Progress	10	Progress	3	Progress	5
Step-back	2	Step-back	2	Step-back	4
Sin	1	Process	1	Revealing	1
Normal Phenomenon	1			Sadness	1
Pain	1			Mistake	1
				Beautiful Mistake	1

E4: To me written error is a/n _____.
(Please use an adjective.)

Freshman		Junior		Senior	
Discouraged	23	Discouraged	10	Discouraged	19
Pleased	6	Pleased	5	Hopeless	4
Incapable	3	Incapable	4	Nothing Special	3

Happy	2	Progressing	3	Stupid	2
Progress-needed	2	Nothing Special	2	Ability Insufficient	2
Normal	1	Self-examined	2	Unhappy	1
Hard-Working Needed	1	Education Needed	1	Piteous	1
So So	1	Disappointed	1	Unavoidable	1
Nothing Special	1	Distressed	1	Doubted	1
Disappointed	1	So So	1	Sad	1
Careless	1	Worried	1	Self-blamed	1
Challenge	1	Confidence Needed	1	Awful	1
Paralysed	1	Hard-Working Needed	1	Incapable	1
		Normal	1	Improvement Needed	1
				Extremely Disable	1

Appendix 6: The Transcript of the Interview

Y: Students prefer to write something about themselves, mostly about descriptive articles. The topics they choose are always different from those in the entrance exam. Is that one reason that students make errors because they're not familiar with the topics?

L: It might be.

C: If they are offered choices in the entrance exam, they will choose what they are familiar with. As to the arguments, they may be lack of vocabulary, or logical thinking, which will lead to their errors. Or they are not taught by teachers to write arguments.

Y: Should the topics of the entrance exam fit what students' need? I mean the compositions should be descriptive mostly.

C: I think it should be balanced. Both should be taught.
Y: Most students would think how to write individually when knowing the topic. The seldom ask teacher for clarification or discuss it with their classmates to get more ideas.

C: Did you give students time to discuss in class?

Y: Sure, I did.

L: Is collaboration learning necessary in writing?

Y: No, not necessary...but they can get more ideas if they collaborate.

C: I think it depends on individual learning style, if time is quite limited in one period, how can they get extra time to discuss with others?

L: Yes, that's right!

C: If a teacher had already explained a topic quite clearly, then there is no need for students to ask more. So, it may be possible that the lower group needs more exploitations than the higher group.

Y: No, the higher group would ask more for explanations than the lower group.
L: Teacher's explanation is clearer and more detailed than students' discussion.

C: I think the problem of time limit is quite crucial. Students have time pressure. They have to submit the final draft before the end of the period... I don't think they would spend time discussing together.

Y: If students ask you how to spell the words, will you tell them directly or ask them to look up in the dictionary?

C: That's no problem.

L: Tell them.

C: If the word has been taught, I tell him to consult the dictionary. If it's difficult, I will tell him.

Y: Sometimes, I feel if I tell one student how to spell a word or how to write a sentence, then I would feel guilty if I don't help others. You know sometimes students are quite lazy.

Y: I wrote the outline in high school. I believe it helps me to develop more easily.

L: It depends on the length of the writing. Student's writings are usually quite short, there is no need to make an outline.

Y: Is outline helpful?

L: Yes, it is.

Y: Outline helps them to think logically and organise it well.

L: I will control students' word number in each paragraph. Don't write too many words.

Y: In the statistics, students usually don't write an outline. Perhaps it's due to the time limit.

C: Yes, I believe so.

C: A well-organised outline is totally useless if the final draft is not completed within time limit.

C: But an outline will help them to know what they are going to write in each paragraph, and that can avoid fragment writing.

C: One of my students asked a Chinese-teaching teacher how to write an English composition and it cause a big trouble. And he went to see his foreign writing teacher and said that's what my Chinese teacher said how to write a composition. The foreign teacher blamed the Chinese teacher for misleading. But the Chinese teacher is so innocent. An English composition stresses the importance of a topic sentence. It is so different from Chinese composition. The Chinese teacher suggested that student to write all the other what he wants to say and then summarise all this sentences in one sentence. This is the topic sentence and place it in the beginning in each paragraph. Our foreign teacher blamed it for misleading.

Y: In Chinese writing, the more you write, the more grades you will get mostly. But it's different from English writing.

C: That's right.

Y: Originally, I thought our students would mostly translate what they are going to write from Chinese into English, but according to the statistics, the ratio is not as high as I expected.

C: So do I. My first reaction is that it's perhaps due to they don't have enough time to translate.

L: Maybe their teachers ask students not to do so before. If they want to improve more quickly, they have to learn to write in English directly.

Y: Some English teachers would suggest their students to write some Chinese sentences first and then translate them into English to make it a short English composition if they do not know how to write an English composition. Do you believe it helpful or not suitable for students?

L: But, students do not have enough input to write what they think directly in English.

Y: I'm afraid that their English compositions translated directly from Chinese would not be understood by native-speakers.

L: That's right! If we read each word student wrote separately, we know what it means. But if we combine the words students wrote together, I don't know its meaning at all.

C: English compositions written by Taiwanese students only can be understood by Taiwanese teachers, not native-speaking teachers, hahaha…(laugh)

Y & L: Hahaha… (laugh)

Y: "Don't fish in the water"…and so on…we Taiwanese teachers can guess its meaning, but not foreign teachers.

C: Yes…in China Post, there is a section telling students how to write an English composition. It lists two different versions on a page. One is about Chinese-laden translation and the other is more correct version and more acceptable.

L: Yeah…right…right…!

C: I cut these paper down everyday and post them on the board at classroom and ask students to read them everyday.

Y: When student come across unknown vocabulary, seldom do they ask teachers, they either look up in the dictionary or find another word to replace it.

Y: When I was a student, I seldom asked teachers, either. But, now students are too lazy to look up the dictionary.

C: Yes, I think so...some of my students just raise their hands and wait for my answers.

L: Maybe they think the answers coming from you (teacher) is more correct and you are the person to correct our writings.

Y: That's possible...right!

L: Yes, they are too lazy. Even they have already got the answers by themselves, they also want to ask you for confirmation.

Y: In some Asian countries, in a writing class, the teacher's only job seems to write down the topic on the blackboard and then the rest depends on students themselves. Teacher's job is over after writing the topic. My English teacher did that to us before.

L: But my English teacher would let use read some model writings first, and give us more time to write it.

Y: Did you copy that modeled writing or change some of it or…?

L: I would create my own.

Y: Some teachers just ask their students memory some patterns and then fit in some words…then an English writing is finished.

C: Yes…hahaha... (laugh) 5 major patterns…

Y: Indeed, just fit in words, then you finish your writing no matter which topic…
It's so magic…!

C & L: Hahahaha… (laugh)

Y: Most students think grammar is very important. We were taught grammatical errors were forbidden before…

L: Right.

Y: In Edge's book, she does not stress so much in grammar. She said we should not expect our learners to be error-free. Communicating is more important.

L: It should depend on what kinds of errors, isn't it?

Y: Yes, we know we only have to pick up major errors and let students find out other minor errors. But you know we all pick up each error for students.

L: Yes…it's our job.

Y: Some books said if we pick up each error, it would hurt students' dignity.

L: It depends on their age.

C: Right, it also depends on students.

C: If a writing is from a group, then I would correct it in detail…but if each student has to submit a writing, I will tell students I won't pick up each errors. Otherwise, correcting 150 writings each week, I will be exhausted.

C: When I first used this method to correct students' writing without any advanced notice for students. You know what…a student came to me so happily just because she thought I missed some her errors. And even she said if she could point out where the error is, she wanted me to give her more marks…

Y & L: Hahahaha… (laugh)

C: Hahaha…, in the beginning, she said to me "Madam, if you make an error in correcting my writing, how many extra marks can you give me?" I didn't understand what she was talking about at that time. She said you did not pick this, this and this error for me…now I find them, give me some extra marks. Of course, after this, I explained to the whole class "I don't pick up each error not because I'm not able to find it but I want you to find them by yourself." Students do care if you don't correct each error…

Y: Students always feel that if teacher does not pick up each writing error, then s/he is not responsible.

L & C: Right…they think so…

Y: Hummm…"coherence", if we translate their writing into Chinese, it's very coherent but the problem is this English writing is not coherent in itself…
Y: Maybe they think first in Chinese and then translate it into English.

L: That's the problem of grammar. Chinese grammar is different from English one, and if you translate one into another forcibly, it would become quite incoherent.

Y: Sometimes, when I read a writing I find its grammar is good enough but actually I don't know what it means…at all.

C: Hahaha… (laugh)

Y: They will use another word to replace his/her original meaning but don't consider their difference, so it would cause misunderstanding for teachers.

L: Teachers need more training…

C: Yes…

Y: Most students believe that the layout or handwriting should be very beautiful in writing.

C: We have been educated to write clearly and beautifully since we're students.

Y: When you're correcting writings, do you have "expression/favored marks" on good handwriting?

C & L: I do…I do…

L: It would influence me if I can understand the words directly or not.

Y: It seems that girls have better handwriting than boys.

C: No…not at all.

L: It's all the same…some girls' handwriting is very ugly, too.

Y: Clear handwriting is very important to teachers.

C: Sure.

L: As far as I am concerned, if a writing is good but with a terrible layout or handwriting, I would be annoyed and even identify them as errors.

Y: That makes sense. Sometimes teacher say it an error just because of awful handwriting.

L: Right...right…and when student comes to see me, I will say it's obviously an error because I cannot read it clearly.

Y: The higher group seem to check their grammar less than the lower group. Maybe they are confident.

L: Maybe they are paralyzed.

Y: The lower group is more afraid of their errors.

L: Right…besides, the higher group has more assignments to write and more exam pressure. They don't focus on one thing with too much effort particularly.

C: I ask students to check their grammar and spelling after writing.

Y: I don't think students would check the coherence always after writing.

C: It's because of their low level. They are unable to detect it.

Y: Usually, we don't think our writing is incoherent, we all clearly know what we are writing.

C: Right, they write down what they think …and believe that's correct no matter how many times they check its coherence. For a student, it's difficult for himself/herself to detect his/her own coherence error.

L: Yes, they check the coherence but only read it once and mostly believe that's exactly what s/he wants to say.

Y: So, should they have to exchange their writings with classmates and let another student find out the errors?

C: Are they able to do this task?

Y: Yes, students do check their writing, but seldom can they detect where went wrong.

C: It's because of different definition of "checking".

Y: That's right. By "checking", we hope our students can detect some errors after writing but they simply read it through...That's it!

C: Yes, they consider "checking" as "reading" it once.

Y: Most students will submit a revised one, not the first draft.

L: Yes, they should not submit their first draft.

C: But, the problem is that they do not have enough time to revise it and then re-written it.

L: That's true.

Y: It seems that nearly all the students will very care about their grades when getting their writings back.

C: Right...that's what they need.

L: Yeah...

Y: Do we need give a mark on student's writing?

Y: If we suppose a writing is a work expressing one's own idea, then what does the "mark" mean actually? Does it mean the marks of "grammar" of "meaning"?

C: Synthetic, general...I will say both.

Y: Some propose there should be no marks on one's writing. But I think the problem is that in Taiwan, marks in a writing is requested and a criteria for accessing students' writing ability.

C: Right.

Y: So, should we give two different marks on a writing: one is for grammar and the other is for meaning?

C: That can be!!

L: It's very difficult to evaluate...

Y: Or our mark is only for the meaning of their writing, because we have a grammar class and we can test their grammatical knowledge on the grammar class. The writing class is used to test their ability of developing meaning and thinking.

C: Yes, can give it a try.

Y: I believe students would always wonder what the "marks" they got represent for?
Do they mean their grammatical ability or writing ability? They will think "I get the low grades, is it the error from my grammar or my thinking?"

C: I don't know if you asked them how many students would look at their errors? Because many students would dispose the writing once they know their grades.

Y: Definitely…they do so quite often.

C: The same mistake would certainly re-appear… I've tested it before. I used some exactly the same questions for the mid-term exam and the final exam to test if they have learned something from their errors in the mid-term exam. And I even warned them in advance if the same question is done wrong again, I would deduct scores double. I've calculated it, nearly two thirds of 50 students make the same error.

C: What's the use for "correction" ? So, since that, I would not give students correct answers after any exam.

C: I don't want to do that stupid job again!

Y: Yes, if correction does work, then no body will make errors after being corrected...but it's not true at all...people still keep making errors and even the same errors. So, does remedial teaching work?

L: It's of no use.

C: It depends on teaching methods. Certainly, we cannot use the teaching method.

L: Once I asked my students to memorise 5 questions because they would appear in the exam...but it's no use at all...There are still many students answering them wrong.
L: I said again I would re-test it but it's still the same. Many errors ...

C: So, we teachers always say don't do such "unhealthy" job, it will decrease our life span. One of my colleagues is quite angry at correcting the same errors...even go crazy!!

Y: The answer in the second question is different from the first one. Few people would look at errors first but most of them would correct their errors directly.

L: I think it means different. Those who would correct their errors perhaps are the people who would look at their errors first when getting back the writings.

C: This second question is contextualised one...you have supposed they have focused on their errors already... and once they noticed them, they would correct them. But the first one is different. So, in the explanation, you have to clarify this.

L: Yes, "careless focusing on errors".

Y: It shows that Chinese influences their writing according to their responses, over 60 %.

L: Something like grammar.
C: I think Chinese would influence their English grammar based on their current level.

Y: You mean it's something like the third singular plural "S", because there is no such rule in Chinese, so students would make this error quite usually?

C: That's right! And "tense". It's the most obvious...and

clauses...adjective clauses, independent clauses...there are too many. They are different from Chinese in structure. But, some can be learned very fast while others cannot be learned by students at all no matter how hard you try.

L: The low-proficiency students cannot make it!

Y: Do you believe the higher similarity two languages have, the easier they can be learned? Or, the less, the easier they can be learned?

C: The more, the easier, I believe. But I read an article before, which says if there is a big difference existing in two different languages, contrarily, it's much easier for students to acquire it. This is mentioned in a book about error analysis. The article mentioned Germany, English and Spanish. It compares the pronunciation between English and Spanish, and compares English and Germany in grammar. They have some huge differences to some degree. It also compares other language and then concludes that the difference does not mean it difficult to learn.

Y: Sometimes, just because of the obvious difference, then it becomes very impressive and thus it's easier to learn it.

Y: As a Chinese speaker, which language is easier for you to learn? English or Japanese?

L: It's difficult to say which…because the time we learn is different and so is the purpose. But when I read Japanese, I have a sense of familiarity; however, when I'm very very tired, I cannot read English at all even if I know English.

Y: Yes, it seems we have our eyes open but without any input at all.

Y: Oh…there are nearly 90% students think their errors come from their insufficient English knowledge.

C: Yes, quite high…nearly 90%.

Y: Does this imply that we, English teachers, do not teach our students well?

C: Students' insufficient proficiency does not represent teachers'… (hummmm)not enough.

C: I think… yes... teachers have some responsibilities but learning should not be the teacher's job only.

Y: Does it mean we, teachers, are not good mediators, we don't mediate students.

C: But different cultures have different backgrounds.

L; Yes, different cultures…

C: In our culture, students depend on us too much.

Y: If a student says to you that "I make errors because my knowledge is poor."?

C: Then let it be…hehehe (laugh)…ask him/her where s/he goes wrong and then improve it. Because their errors may come from their poor vocabulary, thinking or other…They should do this step by step. Don't rush.

C: I always say to my students what learning a language needs is not a genius, but efforts. It's not easy to learn a language perfectly. But everyone can "learn" it.
That's my teaching philosophy.

Y: "There is no student who cannot learn."

C: Exactly…

Y: Hummmm…writing skills…nearly all the three groups have the same proportion. I'm not sure if high school students know any writing skill jus like we do…

C: No, probably they have no idea of it…maybe because the length of their writing is very short.

Y: Yes…time is up or writing is done when they start to apply any writing skill…hahaha…

C: hahaha… (laugh)

Y: I asked them if "slip of pen" would result in errors.

L: Sure, certainly.

Y: There are quite a few students who believe so…uhmmmm…

Y: So, will you remind you students always check their spelling all the time?
L: But when an idea comes out of my mind, I will keep on writing and check the spelling at last.

Y: You know sometime it's quite a pity that a student write quite well but there are too many mis-spelling, slip of pen, which deduce their marks.

Y: The affective factors…the proportion is not as high as the previous ones, but the lower group have a high percentage.

C: Ummm… They're not familiar with writing.

L: The lower group just come into a new learning environment and get nervous more easily.

Y: Yes, the higher group are paralyzed. They have no affection now…hahaha…

Y: I ask them to rank the frequency order of their errors. All the three groups rank the "insufficient knowledge" as the first place.

C: Ummm…Ummm…

L: So the least possible one influencing their errors is affective factors…??

Y: Right!

Y: Look at this question, over 90% students hope their teachers to pick up their each error…quite high…

C: HaHaHaHa…

Y: Don't you feel tired if picking each error up???

L: When I'm reading their writings, yes I do pick up each error.

Y: It seems compulsory.

L: Right, when were students, we also thought correcting each errors was teacher's job.

Y: So, the answer is not surprising at all.

L: The tradition has been deeply-rooted already.

Y: If we don't correct each error, s/he will think I don't like to read the writing.

C & L: Yes.

Y: So, this is the difference between different cultures.
Y: They also don't like teachers only to give them hints about where they make errors...they don't like circles, abbreviations, … something like that. They expect teachers not only to detect their errors but also provide right answers. Look at the proportions...the same, amazingly high.

C: HAHAHAHA… (laugh loudly)

Y: Yes, over 90% students hope so…

L: Over…

L: They think "the more a teacher does, the better; the less a student has to do, the better."

Y: Right! We all had the same expectations when we were students.

Y: Look at the next question, most of them don't like it when teachers only correct major errors.

C: I can tell…hahahaha (laugh).

L: Hahahaha…it's all the same...

Y: I think students are lazy.
L: I don't think they know what the major errors are.

Y: That's right!

L: They think error is an error no matter it's major or minor.

Y: Exactly, in the entrance exam, no matter which kind of error, they're equal… all errors will be deduced from grades fairly.

Y: What do you think the result will be in the question "I hope teachers can offer me more chances to correct my errors by myself"?

C: HAHAHAHA… (loud laugh)

C: I can guess without seeing the results…hahahaha…

L: It's all the same.

Y: Hummmm…half students hope their teachers to take all responsibilities in correcting but half don't…I think there is a problem in this question…I think we have to ask students why they think so by interviewing them…otherwise, who should be responsible for correcting??

C: Hummmm…
Y: How about "peer correction"?

L: Is this applicable in Taiwan??

C: Most of them do not want their classmates to correct their writings.

L: I think students don't want their classmates to know they have errors in writings; besides, I don't believe they are able to do so.

C: Right! Those are two deadly drawbacks in "peer learning". Don't hope others to see my shortcomings and do not trust each other.

L: I think peer learning depends on subjects. History or geography, I think peer learning is fine.

Y: Yes, in writing, students are afraid of being detected errors other than by their teachers.

C: Because we are competitive among each.

Y: Quite competitive. Right.

Y: "Your one error is one extra mark on me." Opportunities to enter university are fixed and each is so competitive to get it! If you make errors, which means I get more chances then you to enter university.

L: "Peer learning" should be applied in the very beginning stage of learning, not in the middle stage or not in a competitive stage.

C: Yes, that's right. They can know what is "trust" earlier.

L: Peer learning also depends on students' ages.

Y: Yes, I tried to do peer correction in the senior group. But it's awful…what they care is the period is ending soon or they can only detect minor errors.

C: Yes, it's related to proficiency as well. This needs training. I think so.

Appendix 7: A Sample of Essay Corrected

My Millennium Wish

In this new year, there are many wishes waiting for me to finish. But most of them that I want to finish is pass the JCEE, and go to the college. And Then I can solve, and do what I want to do — to be free. Because In the passed year, I always studied, studied, and still studied every day. It made me feel the life very dull. So, as long as the mean time passes, I want to release my emotion and go abroad to play with Mom. Although I have many unknown challenges and troubles to face, I still believe that "As long as I am waking, I have a lot of chances to work out them.

Good Conclusion! I agree with you
Wish you good luck!
Be careful about your collocations.
Avoid writing with Chinese ideas.

實踐大學數位出版合作系列
語言文學類　AG0064

高中生英文寫作錯誤分析與探究
An Analysis of Written Errors in Taiwanese
High School Students' Compositions

作　　者	楊文賢
統籌策劃	葉立誠
文字編輯	王雯珊
視覺設計	賴怡勳
執行編輯	林秉慧
圖文排版	劉逸倩　羅季芬
數位轉譯	徐真玉　沈裕閔
圖書銷售	林怡君
網路服務	徐國晉
法律顧問	毛國樑律師
發 行 人	宋政坤
出版印製	秀威資訊科技股份有限公司
	台北市內湖區瑞光路583巷25號1樓
	電話：(02) 2657-9211
	傳真：(02) 2657-9106
	E-mail：service@showwe.com.tw
經 銷 商	紅螞蟻圖書有限公司
	台北市內湖區舊宗路二段121巷28、32號4樓
	電話：(02) 2795-3656
	傳真：(02) 2795-4100

2006 年 7 月
BOD 一版
定價：280元

讀　者　回　函　卡

感謝您購買本書，為提升服務品質，煩請填寫以下問卷，收到您的寶貴意見後，我們會仔細收藏記錄並回贈紀念品，謝謝！

1. 您購買的書名：＿＿＿＿＿＿＿＿＿＿＿＿＿＿＿＿＿

2. 您從何得知本書的消息？

　　□網路書店　□部落格　□資料庫搜尋　□書訊　□電子報　□書店

　　□平面媒體　□朋友推薦　□網站推薦　□其他＿＿＿＿＿＿

3. 您對本書的評價：(請填代號　1.非常滿意 2.滿意 3.尚可 4.再改進)

　　封面設計＿＿　版面編排＿＿　內容＿＿　文/譯筆＿＿　價格＿＿

4. 讀完書後您覺得：

　　□很有收獲　□有收獲　□收獲不多　□沒收獲

5. 您會推薦本書給朋友嗎？

　　□會　□不會，為什麼？＿＿＿＿＿＿＿＿＿＿＿＿＿＿＿＿＿

6. 其他寶貴的意見：＿＿＿＿＿＿＿＿＿＿＿＿＿＿＿＿＿＿＿＿＿

　　＿＿＿＿＿＿＿＿＿＿＿＿＿＿＿＿＿＿＿＿＿＿＿＿＿＿＿＿

　　＿＿＿＿＿＿＿＿＿＿＿＿＿＿＿＿＿＿＿＿＿＿＿＿＿＿＿＿

　　＿＿＿＿＿＿＿＿＿＿＿＿＿＿＿＿＿＿＿＿＿＿＿＿＿＿＿＿

讀者基本資料

姓名：＿＿＿＿＿＿＿＿＿＿　年齡：＿＿＿＿　性別：□女　□男

聯絡電話：＿＿＿＿＿＿＿＿　E-mail：＿＿＿＿＿＿＿＿＿＿＿

地址：＿＿＿＿＿＿＿＿＿＿＿＿＿＿＿＿＿＿＿＿＿＿＿＿＿＿＿

學歷：□高中(含)以下　　□高中　　□專科學校　　□大學

　　　□研究所(含)以上　□其他＿＿＿＿＿＿＿＿

職業：□製造業　□金融業　□資訊業　□軍警　□傳播業　□自由業

　　　□服務業　□公務員　□教職　　□學生　□其他＿＿＿＿＿

To：114

台北市內湖區瑞光路 583 巷 25 號 1 樓

秀威資訊科技股份有限公司　　　收

寄件人姓名：

寄件人地址：□□□

(請沿線對摺寄回,謝謝!)

秀威與 BOD

BOD（Books On Demand）是數位出版的大趨勢，秀威資訊率先運用 POD 數位印刷設備來生產書籍，並提供作者全程數位出版服務，致使書籍產銷零庫存，知識傳承不絕版，目前已開闢以下書系：

一、BOD 學術著作—專業論述的閱讀延伸
二、BOD 個人著作—分享生命的心路歷程
三、BOD 旅遊著作—個人深度旅遊文學創作
四、BOD 大陸學者—大陸專業學者學術出版
五、POD 獨家經銷—數位產製的代發行書籍

BOD 秀威網路書店：www.showwe.com.tw
政府出版品網路書店：www.govbooks.com.tw

　　永不絕版的故事・自己寫・永不休止的音符・自己唱